LIVIA IN ROME

BRUNA DE LUCA

A MESSAGE FROM CHICKEN HOUSE

Food, family and romance are the key ingredients in this warm-hearted debut from my favourite Scottish–Italian writer! If you like falling in love, delicious food and a touch of family drama, this book is for you! So sit back, relax and bask in the beautiful Italian atmosphere of this heartfelt, sun-drenched love story...

BARRY CUNNINGHAM
Publisher
Chicken House

First published in Great Britain in 2025
Chicken House
2 Palmer Street
Frome, Somerset BA11 1DS
United Kingdom
www.chickenhousebooks.com

Chicken House/Scholastic Ireland, 89E Lagan Road, Dublin Industrial Estate,
Glasnevin, Dublin D11 HP5F, Republic of Ireland

Text © Bruna De Luca 2025
Illustration © Ali Al Amine 2025

The moral rights of the author have been asserted.

All rights reserved.
No part of this publication may be reproduced, transmitted, downloaded,
decompiled, reverse engineered, used to train any artificial intelligence
technologies, or stored in or introduced into any information storage and
retrieval system, in any form or by any means, whether electronic or mechanical,
now known or hereafter invented, without the express written permission
of the publisher. Subject to EU law the publisher expressly reserves this
work from the text and data mining exception.

This book is a work of fiction. Names, characters, businesses, organizations,
places, events and incidents are either the product of the author's imagination
or used in a fictitious manner. Any resemblance to actual persons, living or
dead, events or locales is purely coincidental.

For safety or quality concerns:
UK: www.chickenhousebooks.com/productinformation
EU: www.scholastic.ie/productinformation

Cover design and illustration by Ali Al Amine
Typeset by Dorchester Typesetting Group Ltd
Printed in Great Britain by Clays, Elcograf S.p.A

1 3 5 7 9 10 8 6 4 2

British Library Cataloguing in Publication data available.

PB ISBN 978-1-917171-11-3
eISBN 978-1-917171-12-0

For Bruno and Concetta –
the original Italian love story.

1

If there was a law against treating your own daughter like a foreigner, Ma would've been arrested the minute we landed in Rome. First off, she apologizes to the border control officer for my British passport as if I'm a pineapple pizza she's smuggled into Italy. Then, the second we're out of the airport, she turns the hour-long journey to the hospital into one big guided tour – complete with a history lecture on the bus, a trivia marathon on the Metro, and now, as we walk the last stretch, she's still going.

'Look, Livia!' Ma stops for the millionth time, flinging her arms open at an enormous grassy field dotted with rocks and rubble. '*Il Circo Massimo*. Chariot races, gladiator battles, religious parades . . . this is where it all happened.' Her eyes go dreamy and nostalgic as if she witnessed the events in person.

'Wow, Ma! I know you're old, but I didn't think you were ancient,' I joke.

She tweaks my waist, making me jump. 'Don't be cheeky, *signorina*.'

I laugh and push her hand away. 'Well, get moving and stop treating me like a tourist!'

We're only a short walk from the hospital now, and the tiny river island in the middle of the Tiber where it's been squatting for over four centuries – or so Ma tells me.

I grab my wheelie case and step on to a faded zebra crossing, only to lurch back as a horn blasts in my ear and a whoosh of hot, smoggy air whips my hair across my face. Trembling, I peel the strands from my sweaty skin, just in time to see one of my flip-flops bounce into the other lane and a man on a Vespa yelling '*turista!*' at me, as if 'tourist' is a swearword.

Ma clamps her hand around my elbow and ushers me across the road as if I'm six instead of sixteen. 'How about *I* stop treating you like a tourist, when *you* stop behaving like one. This isn't Scotland, Livia. Traffic moves differently here – you can't just assume people will stop. You have to make eye contact first.'

A sharp-suited man with a manicured beard is waiting for us on the pavement opposite, having cheated death to rescue my flip-flop. I hop-limp towards him and he holds it out to me with the very tips of his fingers, a chevron tyre stripe right down the middle of it.

'Your . . . shoe, miss,' he says in heavily accented

English, clearly deciding I'm a *straniera* – a foreigner – and not one of the chic locals who, I realize now, probably wouldn't be caught dead in flip-flops, even if it is the middle of July. I accept it, burning with embarrassment inside and out.

Ma thanks him, her smile verging on a leer the minute he walks away. 'He is *molto carino, no*? Perhaps he has a son who is just as cute.' She cranes her neck to keep him in her line of sight. 'Would you like me to ask?'

'*Ommioddio*, Ma. Stop, will you?'

Ma can be SO inappropriate. Probably because she has little-to-no human interaction outside of Pa and me. Sometimes I think she set up Caterina's Cat Casa because even *she* knows she's better suited to animals than people.

Pa was too tied up with his wedding shoots to come here with us, which is probably a blessing in disguise. You'd think being older than most of my friends' parents would make them stuffy and old-fashioned, but it's like they try to make up for it by going too far in the other direction. Way too far. Ever since Ma and I booked our flights, she and Pa have been teasing me about all the *bellissimi* Italian boys I'll meet this summer, insisting I'll fall in love and never want to come home – *like all the other foreign girls*. Because that's how they see me. Me! Their own flesh and blood. Foreign.

Well, this is my chance to prove them wrong. On both counts.

I was a little kid the last time I was in Rome, but this city's in my DNA. I know it in the bone-deep way birds know migration routes and salmon swim back to the stream they were born in (and, OK, because I have Google Maps). But mostly, I know it because our house in Edinburgh is a little piece of Italy; the food, the music, the TV channels, the bidet in the bathroom and, occasionally, swathes of home-made spaghetti drying on the clothes horse (only my best friend Isla's allowed round on those days).

My phone signal recovers from its recent stint in the bowels of hell – AKA the Rome Metro in summer – and a message from Isla pops up on the screen. She's sent a selfie of herself and a fluffy Maine Coon captioned 'me and your mum'. I smother a snort of laughter; the resemblance is spot on. Ma's 'embracing her grey', and with her old black box dye fading to orange and her patchy silver roots coming through, she's exactly like the tortoiseshell cat in the photo.

Isla's minding the moggies in their luxury cattery extension while we're away. But even when she's there and I'm here, she's in my head, gushing over boys I know she'd like and, more often, over the glazed fruit tarts in the *pasticcerie* windows. I know her so well; I've got an Inner Isla I carry everywhere.

Another ping. *Have you been to the hospital yet?*

I feel a rush of affection for my friend. Unlike my embarrassing parents, she knows why this trip is so important to me. I haven't seen my Nonna Adelina – Nina for short – since I was six years old, and Isla knows her absence has left a gap in my life – an empty space lurking in the background.

It's no wonder I don't feel like I truly belong in Scotland. There isn't anyone to belong *to*. I'm just stranded on the Isle of Ma and Pa with only a bunch of high-maintenance felines for company.

But Rome ... I inhale deeply, breathing in the river Tiber's earthy scent, the fug of exhaust fumes and hot tarmac mixed in with the tantalizing aroma of food and coffee. Rome will be different.

Nina's here, just over the arched stone bridge up ahead. And while I'm sorry it's taken a slippery floor and multiple fractures to get us here, I'm kind of glad it happened. A family emergency is pretty much the only thing that would have prised Ma away from her precious cattery during the busy summer season. And now I have a chance to be a part of something bigger – part of Nina's life and the business that's been in our family for generations.

2

I can still hear Isla's squeal of disbelief when I told her I'd be working in Nina's bar over the summer. 'But you're barely sixteen!' she'd cried, once she regained the power of speech. 'Is that even legal?'

I had to tell her that Italian bars are basically cafes – somewhere neighbourhood pensioners go to gossip over coffees and pastries. In other words, NOT the trendy venue she'd no doubt been imagining. Still, I can't wait to get behind the counter and impress Ma by copying the coffee art TikToks I've been bookmarking like mad.

Ma grew up in the apartment above and worked at Nina's bar as a teenager, so a small part of me – OK, a big part of me – hopes she'll look at me differently when she sees me doing the things she did, in the city she calls home.

And I want to show Nina I care about my roots and my heritage, too. It isn't *my* fault Ma and Pa's businesses get crazy busy during the holidays, or that they're too boring to let me skip school at other times of the year.

A cool blast of air conditioning shivers over my hot skin as we sweep into the hospital. I unstick my T-shirt from my back and dig around for an extra-large hair tie, the only kind that won't snap under the force of my thick hair. I don't need a mirror to know it's expanded to twice its normal bushiness in this heat.

Ma stops at reception for directions to the ward, then we wrestle our luggage into a small old-fashioned lift and get out on the second floor where 'Geriatrics' is written in large letters on a sign above the doors. Ma snorts. 'Nina will love that.' I remember Pa telling me that, although I came up with the name 'Nina' – Nonna Adelina being too much of a mouthful for my then two-year-old self – Nina made sure it stuck, keen to ditch the grandma title.

Her private room is halfway down the corridor and I swear Ma crosses herself as she pushes the door open – something I've never seen her do – but before I can read too much into it, I see her.

Nina.

Or rather, her toes. They're edged with traces of red nail polish and poking out of a heavy-duty splint that's rigged up to a pulley system. My gaze travels upwards to an elegant, fully made-up face and a nose that's just as 'important' as mine and Ma's. Her skin is textured with sun damage and age spots, but plump and wrinkle-free thanks to the fillers and injectables Ma's told me not to mention. As if I would.

I wipe my sweaty palms on my denim cut-offs, aware of how icky and crumpled I am after travelling, and move to her bedside, my smile slipping slowly off my face the closer I get. Why isn't she smiling back? Why isn't she holding her arms out for a hug? Why isn't she saying anything? I want to stop, but my legs keep moving as if I'm stuck on autopilot. I lean in to kiss her cheek, but Nina shifts slightly and my lips end up brushing the pillow instead. Then my face bursts into flames. That's what it feels like anyway.

'She speaks our language?' Nina asks in Italian, addressing Ma instead of me. I'm still reeling from my botched greeting so this hits me like a double blow. Won't she even speak to me directly?

Pa gets this a lot back home; people talking *about* him and not *to* him, and it makes my blood boil. It's like they think his Italian accent makes him stupid, as if being able to speak a whole other language doesn't count if it's not English. Ma's accent is even stronger, but as long as the cats get their gourmet chicken yoghurts on time she could speak like a Minion and they wouldn't care.

'*Capisci perfettamente, vero,* Livia?' Ma's voice is

measured. I nod at Ma. At Nina. Because I *do* understand perfectly. It would be impossible not to. Even the background noise in our house is Italian, what with Ma and her shouty political debates and Pa editing wedding pics to Italian prog rock from his teenage years – bands with dubious names like *I Pooh* and *Dik Dik*. I understand Italian all right. More than I'd like to, sometimes.

But speaking is . . . trickier.

I'm fine with the day-to-day stuff of family life – what to have for dinner, how much make-up is too much, explaining film plots to Ma – but anything more in-depth is a mash-up; a third language that belongs to my family alone. Even the names I call my parents are a compromise – with Mamma and Papà being too Italian, and Mum and Dad too Scottish.

Nina X-rays me with her espresso-brown eyes, seeing right through me to the fraud inside. '*Eh sì*,' she says softly. 'It is as I suspected.'

For a second, I wonder if I've spoken my thoughts aloud. But nope, I haven't said a single word, which is NOT a good look when you're trying to convince your grandmother you're worthy of your Italian blood.

Nina tuts at Ma. 'You have kept her away for too long, Caterina.'

'And it's wonderful to see you too, Mamma,' Ma deadpans, giving my arm a reassuring squeeze before she sits back down with a long-suffering sigh. I realize it's not just the cattery and my education that have kept her away all this time.

I should say something to break the tension, to show Nina I'm not some nodding idiot who can't say a word in Italian. It's all I ever speak with Ma and Pa. And it's not like I have to give a presentation on astrophysics. But in front of Nina, my mouth is glued shut. I awkwardly drift over to the window, my movements self-conscious, and stare out at the soupy green waters of the river Tiber gushing past on either side of the building.

'We're here to help, you know,' Ma says in a clipped voice.

I watch their reflections in the glass. Nina folds her arms across her chest.

'Help? *Uff!* Be honest, Caterina. You've come to tell me I'm too old to run the bar.'

Ma gestures to Nina's suspended leg. 'Well . . . you can't deny it's become too much for you. You'll be seventy-five years old next month—'

'Which means I'm still seventy-four,' Nina cuts in coolly, smoothing her platinum-blonde hair.

Is it my imagination or did Nina look at Ma's

patchwork bob and shudder slightly? Thankfully, Ma hasn't noticed. She's too busy flailing her hands about.

'Fractures take longer to heal when you're older.'

'Ah! *Bene!*' Nina exclaims. 'So now you are a doctor? You should have told me, Caterina.'

Ma throws her hands in the air one final time. '*Dio*, you just never change, do you, Mamma?'

Yikes. We've been here all of twenty minutes and the gloves are OFF.

I get the sudden urge to leave the room; the coins Pa pressed into my hand when we said goodbye at the airport – leftover euros from an Irish wedding shoot – give me the perfect excuse.

'Ummm . . .' I turn to Nina, practising the Italian word for vending machine in my head before I say it out loud, then stop dead in my tracks.

Nina is smiling at me, actually smiling with her teeth and eyes and everything. My heart lifts as I bask in the warmth of it. Then plummets as if I've missed a step.

Because the smile is aimed at someone else. She's looking past me, not at me.

I follow her gaze to the doorway, where a guy in dark glasses and a moped helmet is walking into the room with a stack of foil-covered food containers and an easy smile.

3

I can't see much of the delivery guy's face, but I'm around enough teenage boys at school to recognize the lanky puppy walk when I see it. A rich, nutty aroma and the comforting hint of cooked pasta wafts into the room alongside him. I hope Nina's ordered food for Ma and me, too – lunch was seven hours and 1,500 miles ago.

Nina sits up and reaches for the containers . . . No, wait . . . she's reaching for—

Huh? My jaw practically unhinges itself when she pulls the delivery driver towards her, grasps his helmet in both hands, and plants noisy kisses on his cheeks.

Now, I *know* the kissing thing is totally normal in Italy, sometimes even when you meet someone for the first time, but . . . Really? Some guy from Uber Eats gets a kiss and I don't?

An indulgent smile lifts the corners of Nina's lips and the pulley creaks gently as she adjusts her position to create a space beside her on the bed. She pats the blanket with one slim, brown, liver-spotted hand. '*Siediti qui, caro.*'

Caro? Dear? A sinking feeling hits the pit of my stomach. This isn't some random food delivery person. And it isn't the arrival of her lunch that's making Nina light up like a glow stick. It's this . . . *boy*. This boy who's removing his helmet and sunglasses as if he plans to stick around. This boy who's getting the warm welcome that should have been mine.

I expect to see my own confusion mirrored on Ma's face, but she's on her feet – correction, on her tiptoes – and . . . *ommioddio* . . . now *she's* kissing him too!

'*Ma non è possibile!*' Ma pulls back to study him. 'It can't be you . . . but you're exactly like your mamma with those big cow eyes!'

Cow eyes? Really, Ma? And how can she know what he looks like when she's smooshing his face in her hands, like he's one of her kitty clients? She's even using her 'cat voice' – all fast and high-pitched and babyish.

I shrivel inside. Ma's cringe-rate is off the scale when she's free to speak her native Italian and not her halting English.

'You remember Giulio, don't you, Livia?' Ma steps back a little, as if she expects me to get in line and kiss him too. I stay where I am, ignoring Inner Isla's suggestive snigger and sly *I will if you won't*. Isn't it enough this Giulio person already has two generations of my family fawning over him? And is enjoying every second of it.

Ma turns to me, her voice coaxing, like she's trying to entice a nervous cat out of its hidey hole. 'Giulio's mamma and I were best friends growing up. She brought Giulio to the bar every time we visited. We even joked you'd get married one day. He was so *adorabile*! But now . . . he is *figo*. Isn't that what the young people say? Like that English word Isla always uses . . . Hot? No?'

I bury my face in my hands; this moment will haunt me for ever.

Nina tuts. 'Giulio has no interest in learning English. And how can they remember? It was ten years ago, Caterina. I barely remember it myself.'

There's an edge to Nina's voice, a sharp one that finds its mark judging by the way Ma slumps back into her seat, her legs immediately twisting together like a rope.

But then she smiles sweetly at Nina. 'Perhaps your memory isn't what it used to be, Mamma.'

Ding ding. Round two!

Giulio clears his throat and, taking cutlery and paper plates from Nina's bedside locker with the ease of someone who's done it a million times before, starts dishing out the pasta. The delicious smell of melted pecorino romano cheese and freshly cracked black pepper fills the room. I groan inwardly – *cacio e pepe*, one of my Top Ten! My traitorous stomach actually gurgles.

Nina's eyebrows twitch. 'What on earth are you feeding her, Caterina? It can't be Italian food. Look how thin she is . . . and pale.'

I bite back a growl of frustration. I just can't win. Here I'm too pale, but in Scotland, when Isla and I go make-up shopping, she matches the first cheap bottle of foundation she picks up, while I have to use all my cash on expensive brands that bother to make deeper olive shades. Or how the other girls in my PE class side-eye me when I'm trying to fight my thick wavy hair into a ponytail. I can tell they're thinking I should just straighten it down. And then there's my nose . . . well, let's just say I've tried contouring, but it's still the first thing people look at when they talk to me, before they ask the dreaded question – 'Where are you from?' A question I just don't know how to answer, at least, not with the same conviction Ma and Pa can – Italy. Or Isla can – Scotland. But me? The answer has slipped down the crack in between.

At Nina's insistence, Giulio passes me a double

helping of bucatini and our eyes collide over the saggy paper plate. Reluctantly, I concede Ma is right. Cow eyes. Definitely cow eyes – all big and dark and shiny with a fringe of poker-straight lashes. The opposite of his hair, I realize, which has rippled waves like the fur of a Devon Rex, and is that sun-kissed shade of brown that probably turns darker in winter.

Staring much? Inner Isla's dry jab pulls me from my thoughts and I snap my eyes shut. I am NOT going to be the swooning *straniera* Ma and Pa think I am. Not in front of Nina. Nuh uh. No way.

After all, I'll probably never have to see this boy again after today. Nina has *me* now. I can bring her lunch, dinner and anything else she needs from now on. And maybe then, she'll like me as much as she likes him.

'I almost forgot!' Giulio takes a spoon from a small plastic bag and hands it to me. 'I brought you this.'

My fingers flex and I almost take it so I can hurl it at his head. I've been twirling pasta longer than I've been able to hold a pencil. Is he actually being serious?

I stab my fork into the creamy dish. Giulio's face is blank and emotionless but I look him dead in the cow eyes as I raise a perfectly coiled forkful to my mouth. Or it would have been perfect, if Nina hadn't picked that precise moment to tell Ma I'm starting Italian classes next week.

When I stop coughing and spluttering, I utter my first full sentence in Italian as the pasta unspools into a gloopy mess in my lap. 'Errr . . . *who's* going to Italian classes?'

Nina winces, and I don't know if it's because of my accent or my table manners.

'Lessons are only in the afternoons, and you have time to settle in first,' she says. 'Giulio found a language school close by so it will be simpler for you.'

Giulio, huh? And what, I'm a *turista* who won't be able to find her way around?

Golden Boy, true to his oh-so-helpful self, hands me a wad of paper napkins for the congealing mass of cheesy pasta in my lap. And – surprise, surprise – he's sneaked the spoon inside them. What is it with this guy?

I gather my courage and attempt another sentence in Italian. 'But I'm here to work at the bar and—'

'Giulio can do that,' Nina interrupts, crinkling her eyes at him, her affection stronger than Botox. 'School closes for three months in summer and he's been helping out since June, haven't you, *caro*?'

Nooooo. Not the bar. Pleeeease not the bar! Doesn't Giulio have a family of his own to suck up to? And I don't want to go to Italian lessons, not after the whole exam prep frenzy of the last few months, and worse to come in sixth form.

I shoot Ma my best *do something* face.

She puts down her fork. 'You really should have spoken to us before doing that, Mamma.'

Nina chews, swallows, and pauses to take a dainty sip of water. 'If Livia wishes to reject my gift of the language of art and history. The language of Michelangelo and Da Vinci. If she does not wish to learn ... or *improve*,' she says, her voice rising over Ma's protests that I *do* speak quite a bit of Italian, 'then, so be it.' She rests a hand on Giulio's forearm. 'Can you inform the school, *caro*? A refund will be impossible now, but perhaps they can offer the place to someone who appreciates it ...'

Ugh. Nina is about as subtle as a sledgehammer. But even though I know what she's doing, it doesn't stop the cold spread of panic in my chest. I don't want her to think badly of me, to think I'm ungrateful.

Giulio's blank expression has morphed into one of pure entertainment. He's enjoying this. And I know without a doubt that, while *I* don't want Nina to think badly of me, this grandmother thief clearly does.

I take a deep breath and try to smile. 'It's not that

I don't . . . I mean . . . Of course I want to . . . That is . . .' Nina's eyes bore into me and I stumble over my words, hating that she'll think I'm proving her point. 'I suppose . . . if it's only afternoons?' I finish pathetically.

'*Dio*, Mamma. I won't let you manipulate my daughter the same way you try—'

A nurse in lilac scrubs walks into the room just as Ma rises angrily from her seat. She freezes in a guilty half-sitting, half-standing position while Nina presses the back of her hand to her forehead and groans weakly.

'I believe it's time for Signora De Angelis to rest now.' The nurse holds the door open, his voice as cool as the air conditioning. 'Perhaps you could make your way outside?'

I get to my feet, mortified by the epic fail of my reunion with Nina . . . and by the rogue strands of bucatini that, having escaped my hasty clean-up, are now slipping on to the floor in a soft, humiliating splat.

Giulio wrinkles his nose at the unsightly stain on my shorts. 'You should probably go and freshen up, anyway.'

As I move towards the door, the reek of drying sheep's cheese trailing behind me, I catch Nina lifting her hand to beckon him closer. She leans towards him, her lips moving in a whisper I can't hear. Whatever she says makes his eyes flick briefly to Ma – quick, sharp and deliberate.

'Livia?' Ma's voice snaps me out of my thoughts.

I hurry after her into the hallway, trying to shake off the embarrassment of Giulio's comment and the unease of their closeness.

4

Ma thinks I'm being paranoid about Giulio's spoon offensive.

He was just being helpful. Our families go back a long way. He lost his own nonna recently.

But it's hard to be sympathetic when Signor Giulio zipped off on a Vespa as cool as a cucumber while I swelter on the Metro, nose glued to a stranger's armpit.

I'm so exhausted when we finally emerge from the underground that I barely appreciate the Instagrammable beauty of Rome's Monti district as we walk through it; the flower-filled balconies, the arty independent shops, the pastel-coloured palazzos and, yep, even a view of the Colosseum at the bottom of the street.

Ma is practically vibrating beside me, dying to point it out.

I put her out of her misery. 'I see it, OK?'

She grins for the first time since leaving Nina and, grabbing my free hand, pulls me around a corner and into a vibrant open space. 'This is Piazza della

Madonna dei Monti.' She says it like she's introducing me to an old friend.

A beautiful octagonal fountain sits off-centre, close to the road. And for one ridiculous second, I imagine dunking myself in it, clothes and all. But that's what a badly behaved *turista* would do.

A group of young people sit on the steps around it – talking and laughing, half-listening to a musician playing an acoustic set – and I wonder if that could ever be me.

'I spent my teenage years on those steps,' Ma murmurs, almost to herself. But instead of oversharing like she normally would, her eyes go wide and unblinking like a cat startled by a sudden noise.

I follow her line of sight and spot a vintage Vespa on its kickstand. It's blue, like Giulio's, and my stomach drops. *Dio, no!* Don't let him be here, too! But then I let out a small laugh. This is Rome, *idiota*! There are a million Vespas. And, anyway, Ma's looking at—

Oh! My laughter cuts short. She's looking at the bar beside it. It's so different from my childhood memories that I check the street sign to be sure. Via dei Serpenti. Yes, it's Nina's bar. But even in the waning light, I can see the once-shiny chrome tables and colourful woven chairs are now dull and tarnished. Faded and fraying.

'I knew things were bad, but . . .' Ma quickens her pace, leading me to an arched wooden door that's rotten and uneven around the edges, the wood blistered and peeling. Above it, a faded sign simply reads BAR.

She wrestles a key into the lock and we pause on the threshold, taking it all in – the mismatched tiles patching up the broken floor like sticking plasters, the cracked leather on the stools, the tarnished mirrored shelving lined with rows of dusty bottles, their labels curling at the edges. The bar looks old – and not in a retro or vintage way, either.

A puddle of water spreads out from under the counter and Ma steps closer, crouching to test it with her fingers. 'Ten years, and Nina still hasn't fixed that leak.' She shakes her head slowly. 'Why don't you go up while I sort this, *amore*?' She waves me towards a door behind the old-fashioned counter. 'And don't even think about pinching the double bed . . . or using up all the hot water in the shower,' she calls as I step into the narrow stairwell.

Great. Now Ma's telling me I stink, too.

I climb the stairs; a memory of sliding down them on my bottom – a pair of Nina's heels dangling from my little feet – slams into me out of nowhere. And upstairs, even in the gloom, the silhouettes of the ceramic ornaments on the hallway dresser are so familiar, they tug at something deep inside me – so vivid, it almost hurts. It's as if they've been frozen in time, waiting for me to come back, for me to beg Nina to let me play with them, like I did when I was six years old.

As I move through the apartment, flicking on lights, other memories float to the surface. But there are things that remind me of our house in Scotland, too – the bidet and washing machine in the bathroom, sachets of camomile tea in the medicine cabinet, a blackened moka pot on the stove, and a living room that's more dining table than anything else. A bubble of hope swells in my chest. The things that feel out of place in Scotland fit right in here. So maybe I can, too.

I find Nina's room with its enormous sleigh bed and a nightstand cluttered with more beauty products than a city centre Sephora, then walk down the corridor to my room – the one that used to be Ma's.

My phone vibrates in my back pocket as I push the door open. I swipe to answer, and Isla's face fills the screen.

'I miss youuuu!' she pouts. 'You've been gone a whole day.'

'I'm just checking out my room. Want to see?'

'Yeah! Flip the camera.'

I switch on the light, surprised to see a collection of trophies and medals on top of the chest of drawers, and football posters all over the walls.

'Wait . . . your mum was sporty?' Isla sounds shocked.

'Err, no . . . I swear none of this was here the last time we stayed.' My eyes land on a huge collage of photos on the wall above the bed. 'Or that.' I kick off my flip-flops – vowing to never wear them again – and climb on to the mattress for a closer look.

My breath catches. The pictures are all of Giulio – younger, but undeniably him. Giulio blowing out candles on a birthday cake while Nina smiles on. Giulio and Nina eating gelato together. Giulio posing with her after a football match. Giulio and Nina. Nina and Giulio.

I squash down the awful feeling that I'm seeing what could have been my childhood right in front of me.

'Aw, who's the cute kid?'

I startle, forgetting Isla's seeing all this too.

'Giulio,' I say through gritted teeth, switching the camera back to me. 'And he's not cute or a kid. He's the same age as us. The photos are old.'

Isla perks up. 'So you know him? Is he . . . Italian?'

I roll my eyes. 'Yes, he's Italian.'

She dips her chin to peek over the top of her glasses. 'Aaaand?'

'And what?'

'Is he . . . *Italian* Italian? You know . . . tanned, handsome, fashionable, dreamy accent—'

'Stop!' I beg, scrubbing her annoyingly accurate description of Giulio from my brain. And here I am worrying about being a walking cliché when Giulio's the very definition of one.

Isla does the tiny clapping thing she does when she's excited. 'So, he is then!'

'I did NOT say that.'

'But you didn't not say it either.'

'Yeah, well, you should have seen Nina with him – it's like he's everything she wants me to be. They've even ganged up to send me to Italian classes.'

'Italian classes? Liv, you literally only speak Italian at home.'

I smile at my friend. 'Isla, you think me offering to empty litter trays for cash or promising Pa I've done my homework before we go out is impressive.'

Isla shrugs. 'Honestly? It is.'

'Yeah, well, I'd still get tongue-tied saying those things in front of Nina.'

'So maybe classes will be good then?'

'Maybe,' I accept. But still . . . what kind of Italian needs to take Italian lessons?

'Hey, you're in the city centre, right? Let me see the view.'

Isla always knows how to get me out of a funk, because when I open the shutters I can't help grinning. The window faces exactly the way I hoped, giving us a glorious glimpse of the Colosseum.

I point my camera towards it. 'Nice, huh?'

'Gorgeous,' Isla says dreamily. 'Utterly gorgeous.'

I'm about to agree, but then I realize she isn't talking about the most famous building in Rome. She's drooling over the boy in the foreground – Giulio, leaning casually on the balcony next door, admiring the blue Vespa below like it's the Mona Lisa.

Ommioddio – seriously? He lives next door? I yank the phone back towards me and slam the shutters closed.

'Oh Liv,' Isla laughs. 'You are so doomed.'

5

Talk about a rude awakening. The first thing I see after groping for my phone in the pitch dark is a dozen Giulios grinning down at me from the collage on the wall, illuminated by the glow of my screen – like he's been mocking me even in my sleep.

I yelp at the time, cursing myself for setting the shutters to wartime blackout mode to block out Giulio's existence. Problem is, these are heavy-duty Italian shutters – they don't let in any heat, any light . . . or any inkling that I've massively overslept and it's practically midday.

I throw on the first outfit I find and thunder downstairs, almost taking Giulio out as I fly through the door connecting the apartment to the bar. He grabs my upper arms to steady me and my skin prickles at the unexpected touch of his skin against mine. He's like a stinging nettle, I think darkly, taking a step back to put some distance between us.

His eyes flick to the wall clock, then to my unbrushed hair and wrinkled T-shirt. 'Nice of you to join us, Scotland.'

Scotland? *Uffa!* Can't he say anything without reminding me I'm an outsider?

It's the first English word I've heard him say, but his Italian accent wraps around it, making it sound warm and tropical. Nina said he's not interested in learning the language. Maybe I can use that. In Scotland, Italian can be a handy secret language. Here, English could be the same . . .

'You missed the breakfast rush,' he adds, nodding towards the dirty cups and plates cluttering the sink area.

I fake an apologetic smile. 'You're right. I should have been here. Why don't you take a break now and come back in, say . . .' I look at the clock, too. 'September?'

I mentally pat myself on the back for saying this in Italian, even if I'm not sure it was entirely correct.

'Livia!' Ma, who has been wiping tables outside, points the nozzle of the spray cleaner at me as she comes back in. 'Behave! Giulio has been a lifesaver this morning. He's even taken Nina her lunch already.'

Great – now Nina will think I'm lazy, as well as a pale misfit who desperately needs Italian lessons.

Giulio moves to the glasswasher but, determined to show him I belong here as much as he does, I snatch an apron from a hook on the back wall and, tying it firmly around my waist, nudge him aside. 'Leave that. I've got it covered.'

Giulio's lips quirk upwards in what I can only describe as a wicked smile as he ever-so-slowly looks me up and down. 'Sure about that? Because, from where I'm standing, it's pretty obvious you don't have anything covered at all.'

I frown in confusion. Then my face flames to the very tips of my ears. *Ommioddio.* I'm wearing one of those novelty aprons I've seen outside tourist shops; the ones that make you look like a naked statue wearing nothing but fig leaves. This one happens to be of a woman.

'A couple of backpackers left it here last week,' Giulio says. 'They're probably long gone, so feel free to keep it ... it'll save you buying your own.'

I fold my arms across my chest, covering myself up and expressing my annoyance in one go.

Uff! I hate this boy. He sounds SO reasonable on the surface, so kind. Thoughtful, even, with his whole *Here, Livia, have a spoon for your pasta. Hey, Livia, why don't you keep that tacky tourist apron? You know, Livia, I'm more than happy to hold the fort and feed your grandmother while you lie in bed.*

Ugh! Well, Ma and Nina might have fallen for his

charm, but I can read between the lines. And it goes something like this: *You're just a lazy turista and you'll never be one of us, Livia. And, by the way, you stink of cheese.*

I resist the urge to do something murderous with the apron strings, and channel my Inner Isla instead. I give Giulio the same slow head-to-toe once-over he just gave me, making sure to look unimpressed – which means ignoring Inner Isla's inconvenient observations about how the apron he's wearing is tied tight enough to show off his swimmer's body, and how he looks like he's stepped right out of a billboard ad for Armani Exchange or some other Italian brand.

'You should get the apron that has Michelangelo's *David* on it. It would be . . . you know . . . a big improvement.' I let the dig hang in the air between us. That particular statue is the symbol of youthful male beauty. But far from being put out, Giulio's cow eyes gleam with mischief.

'Or I could just wear a fig leaf and achieve the same effect.'

'Ha! You wish!'

I spin to face the huge La Cimbali coffee machine on the ledge behind me, and pretend to inspect the dials and switches while my cheeks cool down. The oversized hunk of metal vibrates with a low hum that does nothing to mask Giulio's soft chuckle as he moves away.

'It's so nice to see you two getting along,' Ma murmurs.

My spine stiffens. While Italian is my default with Ma — something she's insisted on since I was tiny — I switch to English so I can insult Giulio freely. 'What? Me get on with that smug, arrogant, rude—'

'OK, OK! *Scusami*.' Ma laughs.

She's not sorry at all. Her lips are pressed together as if she's suppressing a smile, and I just know she's going to tell Pa I couldn't even go a full day in Rome without flirting with some Italian boy — which is NOT what was happening at all.

I'm about to snap back when an elderly *signora* walks into the bar. Ma drops to the floor as if someone's just taken aim at her.

'Wha—?'

Ma holds up a finger and mouths, 'You didn't see me!' Then she crawls commando-style to the door at the end of the counter and disappears upstairs.

I'm still gawping after her when the source of Ma's vanishing trick approaches the counter. Her small head, barrel-shaped body and short skinny legs remind me of a robin, an overgrown one wearing a flowery blouse and knee-length black skirt. Milky blue eyes peer out at me from deep wrinkles. 'Ah, now who is this *bella ragazza*, Giulio?'

I squirm at being called pretty, especially when I rolled out of bed five minutes ago. And why can no one over the age of seventy speak to me directly here?

'*Salve*, Signora Pedretti,' Giulio shouts in her ear. 'This is—'

'*Aspetta!* Don't tell me . . .' She flattens her hand against Giulio's chest, making me squirm a little, then narrows her eyes until they almost disappear. 'I know this girl, don't I? She looks . . . familiar.'

'I don't think we've met before,' I say.

Signora Pedretti claps her hands together. 'Ah, but you are not from here!'

Ouch. Signora Pedretti isn't just my first customer; she's the first person I've spoken Italian to outside of my family and Giulio. And it only took a handful of words for her to clock my accent. My body crumples as I exhale. Maybe I do need those Italian classes after all.

She continues to scrutinize me, then her gaze darts to my nose, and her mouth drops open in recognition. 'Ah! *Dio mio!* You're Caterina's daughter! Where is your mamma? I need to have a word with her.'

'She's upstairs,' Giulio answers.

'She just stepped out,' I blurt, my words overlapping his.

Signora Pedretti arches a brow and I laugh nervously.

'So . . . what can I get you, Signora?'

She studies me for a while longer. '*Eh, vabbè. Un caffè, per favore.*'

I don't ask what kind of coffee she wants. *Un caffè* means one thing, and one thing only – an espresso.

I turn back to the hulk of chrome, a flutter of anxiety in my chest.

'First, make sure the portafilter's clean.' The unexpected sound of Giulio's voice in my ear sends a rash of goosebumps skittering up the back of my neck. I have a definite allergy to this boy, I think, as he passes me a device with a long black handle.

'Then tap it out, wipe it down and fill it with coffee – you'll need to grind some, it's been busy.' He gestures towards one of the many switches, and I follow his instructions, focusing on all the new Italian words I'm learning and trying to ignore his closeness as I tamp down the freshly ground coffee and lock the portafilter into place.

'Now, start the machine.' Giulio points to another switch and pushes his long body away from the counter. 'OK from here? I need to sort out the tables and . . . well . . . you should take full credit for your first *caffè*.'

A rich dark liquid starts flowing into the doll-sized cup and I breathe in the intense, full-bodied aroma. Ahh. Perfect! So why do I get the feeling there's something ominous behind Giulio's words – something lurking between the lines, as usual?

I watch him from under my lashes as I set a tiny saucer and teaspoon on the counter. He's so at home here, trading jokes with the shop owner next door as he restocks the sugar sticks and sweeteners outside. But he keeps glancing over at me and I can't help thinking he's like a tomcat guarding his territory.

I place the espresso in front of Signora Pedretti. OK. It was hardly rocket science, and I didn't get to try any coffee art, but it's a start. A good one.

Signora Pedretti takes a cautious sip, her lips puckering immediately. 'Have you changed coffee supplier?'

'Umm . . . is there a problem?' A twist of anxiety knots my stomach when I spot Giulio's blank expression – I've known him less than a day, but I know that face means he's up to something.

Signora Pedretti puffs out her chest, feathers clearly ruffled. 'It tastes like dirty water!'

Giulio steps forward, all apologetic charm. 'Please, forgive Livia. She must have made the coffee grind too coarse. As you said, she's not from here and still has a lot to learn. Let me make you a proper one.'

I clench my jaw, fighting to keep my cool as he expertly makes another *caffè* – just like he planned all along.

This time, Signora Pedretti takes a sip and smacks her lips. '*Bravo*, Giulio. It is *perfetto*.'

She leans in, mistaking my fury for disappointment. 'You'll get the hang of it, *cara*. Giulio has made countless cups . . . he's never away from the place. Perhaps he'll take some time off now you're here, see his friends.'

'Sadly, my friends are all at the coast or abroad, Signora, enjoying the holiday before school.' He nods in my direction. 'And I think I'm needed here more than anywhere else.'

If Signora Pedretti hears me grinding my teeth down to little stumps, she shows no sign of it as she drains her cup, hops off her stool and calls over her shoulder on her way out. 'My god-daughter Flaminia was saying the same thing, Giulio. She's stuck in the city, too. You two should get together.'

'What do you think, Scotland?' Giulio asks when Signora Pedretti disappears from view. 'Would Flaminia like me . . . or would she find me smug, arrogant and rude?'

I freeze. He heard what I said to Ma. Worse. He *understood* me.

'We can speak in your language if that's easier for you,' Giulio says in perfect accented English. 'At least until you've been to a few Italian classes.'

I could froth milk with the steam coming out of my ears.

That. Is. It. No more English. Not a word. Not with Giulio. Not with anyone. Except Isla, I quickly amend. There's no way I'm surviving this summer without her.

6

Ma tiptoes back behind the counter a short while later like a nervous cat coming into the cattery for the first time, eyes darting. Her shoulders visibly relax when she sees the place is empty.

'It's OK, she's gone,' I tease.

'Hmm . . . who's gone?' She acts clueless but I see the flush creeping up her neck.

'Signora Pedretti . . .' I gesture to where she'd been crawling on the floor twenty minutes earlier. 'You know, that whole thing.'

Ma's phone screen starts flashing, and relief washes over her face – saved by the bell. Only the bell is a loud, repetitive meowing sound. I still can't believe Isla set that ringtone for her.

I drop my hands from my ears as Ma answers, and Pa's face appears on the screen. I lean in so he can see both of us.

The comb-over Pa denies having is blowing about in the wind like an inflatable tube man, the strap of his beloved Leica camera bright against the black shirt he wears to wedding shoots. He's in a field somewhere and strong gusts are playing havoc with the phone's microphone. The whole Italians-talk-with-their-hands thing is in full swing as they try to hold a conversation.

Giulio's been scrolling through his own phone by the counter, but I notice his hand stilling when Ma launches into a rant about the state of the bar and how Nina can't be coping, financially or otherwise.

My nostrils flare. He's definitely eavesdropping.

I'm about to call him out on it, when the dying sputter of a moped engine has him bolting outside to intercept the postal worker. He takes a bundle of letters directly from her hands and quickly rifles through them.

'I'll take those,' I say, fed up with him acting like he owns the place.

But he sidesteps me without even looking up. 'It's just junk, Scotland.'

I turn to stare daggers at his back, and that's when I spot a brown envelope peeking out of his back pocket. The beginning of Nina's name just visible on the fold.

I point an accusing finger. 'Hey, what's that?'

Giulio turns, a smirk tugging at his lips. 'That? That's my backside, Scotland.'

'That's not . . . I didn't . . .' Heat rushes to my face, and Inner Isla chooses that moment to mutter something about it being worth a second glance – traitor.

Ma puts her phone down and leans her elbows on the counter. 'Play nice, *tesoro*. Giulio's just being helpful.'

'It's OK, Caterina. I'm sure Livia didn't mean to be abrupt. It's easy to get muddled when Italian's not your first language. That's what the lessons are for.'

Ooft! A double dig – not only reminding me about my Italian lessons, but insinuating I need them too.

I spread my hands towards Ma in silent appeal – *See what he's like?*

But Ma, missing the subtext as usual, shakes her head fondly. 'I'm afraid you're being too generous, *caro*.'

I bite back the retort on the tip of my tongue and glare at Giulio instead. Generous? Not the word I'd use.

'Aren't we closing for lunch?' I ask, keen to get rid of him.

Many bars here shut during the hottest hours of the day, and I know Nina does too, but Ma shakes her head. 'I need to do a stocktake and see what's what. We may as well stay open.'

But even with the doors flung wide, no one comes in. And as the afternoon drags on, I get a clearer picture of how Giulio's been managing on his own while Nina's been in hospital. The place is dead. So dead, it's only 7 p.m. when Ma announces we're closing early — early for Italy, that is. Back in Scotland, we'd already have shut the doors. And while I'm glad to see Giulio leave, taking his smug comments and irritating smirk with him, I get why Ma's wondering how Nina's getting by.

Ma pushes some buttons on the till and it spews out a receipt. 'It won't take me long to cash up. Want to eat on the terrace tonight?'

'The terrace?' I echo, surprised. I didn't even know there was one.

She raises an eyebrow. 'You haven't been yet? You were desperate to get up there when you were little. We had to watch you like a hawk.'

Memories flash through my mind of a staircase behind a door, and of Nina turning a key and pocketing it.

I climb the steps and find myself on a tiny roof terrace crowded with luscious potted plants and mismatched bits of outdoor furniture. But it's the view that really grabs my attention. I finally get why Pa's so obsessed with Golden Hour. The sun is low in the sky over Rome, its warm light hitting the red rooftops and mustardy-coloured palazzos that are crammed together like Tetris pieces. If it weren't for the intense heat and the sounds of voices and traffic around me, I'd think it was a painting.

A free-standing hammock in striped deckchair colours sits off to one side. It sways invitingly at my gentle push, so I tentatively hoist one leg only to end up doing a bad impression of the splits. It swings sideways as I hop closer with my standing leg, then it's a full thirty seconds before I'm properly inside. It could be the sun, but I am suddenly hot all over and worried that someone in the neighbouring palazzos has seen my awkward moves.

But when I'm finally lying down, my weight supported by the strong fabric, the worries of the day lift away too. Cocooned, one finger poised to FaceTime Isla, I smile to myself. I've found my first Roman happy place – which is good, because I'm not entirely sure I know how to get out of this thing.

I wriggle deeper. Could I sleep out here? Better this than a collage of Giulios staring down at me. My own little escape, far away from that smug, annoying—

'Don't post any more letters to the bar, OK?'

Is that . . . Giulio? At first, I think I'm hallucinating – it's still so hot, and I'm frazzled to the max after spending the whole day with him – but then his voice drifts over again.

'I told you. I'm not alone any more . . . and the daughter mustn't find out.'

My heart thunders in my chest, so loudly I'm afraid the sound will carry like Giulio's disembodied voice. I peer over the edge of the hammock, confirming what my sinking stomach already knows. Giulio's apartment has access to the adjoining roof terrace.

And . . . *ommioddio* . . . what daughter? Does he mean me . . . or Ma?

7

I wake up to Isla's name flashing on my buzzing phone. She's already up and dressed when I answer – the cattery's communal area with its multilevel play spaces and cosy igloos behind her. From the camera angle, I'm fairly certain she's propped me up on a litter box in the sanitation corner.

'Liv! Sorry I couldn't speak last night. Your mum says you're still in bed, but I wanted to catch you before the cat chaos takes over.'

I sit up. I didn't get to tell her about Giulio's shady phone conversation last night because when I called, she was mid-argument with a bouncer accusing her (correctly) of having a fake ID.

'You've spoken to Ma already?' I check the time, worried I've woken up late again. But there's still forty minutes until the bar opens.

Isla rolls her eyes. 'She called five minutes ago to quiz me on the evacuation procedures. Again.'

Yep, that sounds like Ma. 'I wish she had a procedure to evacuate Giulio. He's— *eww!*'

A cat's bottom fills my screen.

Isla scoops the black-and-white tuxedo cat into her lap and scritches him – yes, definitely him – under his chin to keep him still.

'From what I've seen, he's the opposite of *eww*,' she quips.

'Ha ha. Well, get this. I think he's hiding something, but there's no way Ma and Nina will think he's capable of any wrongdoing unless I have proof. I need to find out what he's really up to. I need . . . a plan.'

Isla sits up straighter. I knew this would get her attention. Isla prides herself on being devious, like the time she set up a fake home screen so it looked like we were doing homework instead of gaming, or when she made a copy of the key to the high school greenhouse using a potato mould so we could spend break there in secret.

I quickly fill her in on the letter he swiped from the postie, and the call on the roof terrace. As she listens, I can almost see the calculations taking place in her head. So I'm a bit disappointed when she says, 'Simple. Get close to him. Be his friend.'

I stare at her in silence and she backtracks.

'OK, fine. *Pretend* to be his friend.'

'Err . . . there's a reason I quit drama after one term, remember? I was thinking more . . . spy on him from a distance?'

Isla laughs. 'What distance? From what you've told me, you two practically live on top of each other.'

I feel myself redden at her words, but mercifully Isla doesn't notice.

'There's more to it than that,' she insists. 'I don't like it when people are mean to you, right?'

I think of the boy at school who called me O-Livia Oil when he saw me drizzling a home-made dressing over a sad little salad from the school cafeteria. That was four years ago and Isla still 'accidentally' knocks into him whenever we pass him in the corridor.

'Ye-es,' I say cautiously. 'But I still don't follow.'

'Think about it. If Nina's as fond of Giulio as you say she is, she's not going to like you being mean to him. But if you're his friend, she'll warm to you more quickly. You'd be closer to the action, better placed to find out what he's really up to. And we both know how hot he is—'

'I do no—'

'So it shouldn't be too hard,' she finishes, speaking over me. 'What's that saying your dad uses . . . the flies and the vinegar thing?'

'Umm . . . you can catch more flies with a drop of honey than a barrel of vinegar?'

Cavolo! Why is Isla's reasoning always so . . .

reasonable? Could I really pretend I want to be friends with Giulio? It would take some serious skills to pull it off. But isn't it worth a try if it helps me uncover what he's doing behind everybody's backs, and maybe even find evidence that neither Ma nor Nina will be able to sweep under the Giulio-is-great carpet?

One thing I do know – if I'm going to pull off this charm offensive, I need to look my best.

Maybe it's the water quality in Rome, or Nina's expensive bath products, but as I tuck my tee into my waistband and check myself in the small mirror, I actually don't hate my hair for once. Yeah, there's still an insane dark mass floating around my head, but it's less of a frizzy mess and more light and swishy. It bounces around my face as I hurry downstairs.

I walk into the bar just as Giulio arrives. He freezes when he sees me, a weird expression on his face that has me checking the hem of my maxi skirt isn't tucked into my underwear. No, it's not that. I look at my feet. No, definitely no flip-flops, just plain white canvas Superga trainers; they claim to be 'The people's shoe of Italy', so he can't pick fault with them, right?

I want to scowl but then I remember Isla's advice and switch to a smile instead, hoping it doesn't look the way it feels – like I'm baring my teeth.

Giulio's expression switches from cryptic to very, VERY confused.

Ma reaches over the counter to ruffle my hair. 'Ah, you're up early today! Isn't my daughter *bellissima*, Giulio?'

Then she winks at him. Actually winks! And there's a big cheesy grin plastered to her face, too. Oh no. That look. She's going to be straight on the phone to Pa the minute I'm out of earshot with her 'I told you so's.

Nope. Not happening.

I spear Ma with a reprimanding death stare as I come out from behind the counter. This is one problem Isla didn't consider in her grand plan – how to act friendly towards Giulio without Ma thinking I'm making foreign-girl moves on the cute Italian boy.

As the breakfast rush kicks in, it becomes painfully obvious that Ma and Giulio don't trust me with the coffee orders or the till. Frustrated, I stalk Giulio's every move like a cat chasing a laser dot, waiting for him to grab more post or sneak in another dodgy phone call. But nope – while I'm stuck picking up used toothpicks and getting my face steamed every time I open the glasswasher, I have to endure him chatting and joking with the regulars with an ease I can only dream of.

Just as I'm wondering if the day can get any worse, Giulio announces, 'It'll be lunchtime soon. I'd better take Nina some food.'

And there it is – Nina. He's calling her by the name I gave her when I was little. He's taking something that is rightfully mine. I bite my lip and scrub at a decades-old coffee ring to keep from snapping.

Ma gestures towards the mostly cleared tables. 'There's hardly any customers, I can manage on my own. You should go too, Livia. You're always complaining you don't see enough of Nina.'

Giulio makes a strangled noise, clearly as horrified as I am at the suggestion, but I still throw a smile his way before twisting my head slightly to shoot Ma 'A Look' – with capitals. 'Or,' I force the words through a gritted-teeth smile, 'maybe you and I could go, and Giulio could stay?'

Ma bats my suggestion away with a wave of her hand. 'Once a week is enough for me. I'll stick to Sunday lunches and leave the other days to you. I'm sure she'd rather see you two, anyway.'

A hint of frustration stirs inside me. We came all this way and she only wants to see her once a week? Why exactly are things so off between them? I've always accepted Ma's excuses about the cattery and Pa's work, and their not wanting to take me out of school, but there's definitely something deeper going on, something she's not telling me.

Inner Isla, in the meantime, is practically elbowing me in the ribs. *Remember the plan. Go. With. Giulio!*

I take a deep breath and, struggling for a tone that's neither too friendly (for Ma to misinterpret) or too unfriendly (for Giulio to *correctly* interpret), I say, '*Va bene*, I'll go to the hospital. I missed out yesterday and I want to see as much of Nina as I can.'

A rustling noise at the entrance grabs our attention and Signora Pedretti's head pops into view, leaning in as if she's been lurking just out of sight. Her smile is a touch victorious as she looks at Ma. 'I heard you were back!'

Ma freezes, like she's in *Jurassic Park* and has been told to stay still to avoid being detected by carnivorous dinosaurs. But realizing how ridiculous she looks, she loosens up and forces a polite smile. 'Signora Pedretti, how lovely to see you again. You met my daughter, Livia, yesterday?'

Signora Pedretti nods. 'I knew she looked familiar. Such a strong . . . resemblance.' Her milky little raisin eyes linger on the big Roman monument in the middle of my face.

'*Forza!* You two.' Ma shoos Giulio and me towards the door. 'Don't keep Nina waiting.'

Giulio hesitates, wanting to protest, but Ma practically shoves us outside.

On the street, we exchange a glance that, for once, has nothing to do with the tension between us, and I decide now's a good time to kick-start my fake attempt at being friends.

'Well, *that* was weird! It looked like Signora Pedretti was lying in wait for Ma.' I start walking towards the Metro station, but Giulio catches my wrist and pulls me back. I stare at his hand, at his long fingers, momentarily stunned by the warmth of his skin against mine.

'Not that way.' He tugs me gently to the left before releasing me, and I find myself standing next to his blue Vespa.

'Wait!' My eyes go wide. 'You want us to go on that?'

The smug smirk is back with a vengeance. 'It's how we locals travel around here, Scotland.'

Dio! Why is his every comment designed to push my buttons?

Inner Isla swoops in. *Zip it and channel Audrey Hepburn, Liv.*

My stomach flutters at the thought of riding this iconic scooter across Rome. I mentally trace the route; it'll take us past the pillars of the Roman

Forum and the imposing architecture of Piazza Venezia, then across the city to Isola Tiberina. Definitely an improvement on the concrete walls and sweaty armpits of the Metro.

And it doesn't look like I have a choice anyway.

Giulio fishes out a second, smaller helmet, decorated with cute anime stickers, from under the Vespa's seat. As I take it, a sudden thought crosses my mind – does he have a girlfriend? I mean, he's probably not muscling in on everyone's grandmother, so with a big stretch of the imagination, I suppose it's possible *someone* might be into him.

8

The Vespa saddle looks long, but by the time I climb on behind Giulio – with only slightly more dignity than I managed the hammock – and scoot right back against the grab rail, we're still uncomfortably close. I'm hyper-aware of every point of contact and wish I'd worn jeans instead of this skirt, because it feels like there's not enough material between us.

The engine whines as Giulio accelerates into the road, tilting us sharply. I grab his sides, feeling hard muscle under my fingers before I pull them away and grip the saddle instead. I've never actually been pressed up against a guy before and I try to keep away from him, but every bump in the road shoves me closer, like the city itself is determined to throw us together. It's impossible to avoid touching him. I can even feel the heat of his back through his shirt as we speed through the bustling streets, past historic landmarks and crowded piazzas, each corner and curve offering a snapshot of Rome's street life and fancy buildings. The city's beauty almost distracts me from the awkwardness. Almost.

When we reach Isola Tiberina, I slide off the saddle on shaky legs, trying not to think about having to do this all over again on the way back. Giulio pulls the Vespa on to its kickstand, and we head to the trattoria to pick up our food. It's the only building besides the hospital, a church and a small pharmacy on the tiny island, as if access to restaurant-quality food is just as important as religion and healthcare here. And judging by the delicious smell of the carbonara and the mouth-watering aroma of sage and prosciutto wafting from the *saltimbocca* we pick up for ourselves and Nina, I can totally see why.

Inside the hospital, we walk along the corridor side by side and I rack my brain for friend-type questions that might get me close to the information I'm looking for. 'So, you've been working at the bar for a while then?'

Giulio's step falters a moment. 'I suppose. Nina's needed me more, recently. Even before she broke her leg.' He doesn't meet my eyes, but I detect a challenge in his voice when he says, 'She's like family.'

I'm not sure what to make of that. He sounds sincere . . . like he actually cares about her. But does he? Would he be creeping around stealing her letters and making dodgy phone calls if that were true?

I brace myself as we reach Nina's door. I know I'll have to speak. I can't keep showing up without saying a word, but the thought of messing up my Italian in front of her is paralysing. It's bad enough watching Giulio scrunch his face when I talk, as though understanding my less-than-perfect accent requires all his effort.

I hover awkwardly by the door, feeling like an intruder, as Giulio leans in to kiss Nina's cheek – a mistake I won't be making this time. I watch their easy familiarity, a pang of jealousy tightening in my chest – not just for their closeness but for the effortless way he fits into her world and into this city.

Giulio straightens and Nina's eyes meet mine. It could be my imagination, but her smile dims slightly. 'Livia. You woke up in time today.'

'Yes, Giulio was kind enough to bring me along,' I reply, forcing myself from the doorway and burying the hurt where neither of them can see it. It almost kills me to say something nice about Giulio in front of her, but what if Isla's right? What if the way to Nina's heart is through him?

'He is a *bravo ragazzo*, isn't he?' Her face splits into a wide smile when Giulio places the food on the overbed table in front of her. She inhales deeply.

'*Saltimbocca!*' She pats Giulio's hand. 'How did you know that's exactly what I wanted?'

Giulio's eyes flick to me and I read their silent message. I might be Nina's family, but I don't know her like he does. I don't share their history. I don't know her taste in food. But he does.

'Can you get the cutlery?' Giulio asks casually. Too casually. 'It's spaghetti, so a fork for me and Nina . . . and whatever you need.'

Easy, Livia. Easy, Inner Isla warns. I thrust my head into the cabinet and scowl at Giulio in secret, only coming out when I'm back in control. But he's ignoring me anyway, chatting with Nina, one hand hooked casually into the back pocket of his jeans. The same pocket where I saw him stuff that mysterious letter.

It's payback time.

'Didn't you pick up some post for Nina yesterday?' I ask brightly.

There. A definite shiftiness in Giulio's eyes. He narrows them slightly before tutting. 'Nothing to worry Nina about. She's here to recover, remember?'

I flush at the reprimand in his words.

Mannaggia! How does he always twist things so that I'm the bad guy?

'But you can tell her about that silly mishap at the bar,' Giulio adds. He's getting me back – does he know I'm suspicious about the missing letter?

'What mishap?' Nina asks sharply.

I hesitate, partly because I really don't want to tell her, and partly because I'm scared I'll mess up my accent or get the verb endings wrong.

Giulio, of course, can't wait to fill her in. 'Oh, you know what Signora Pedretti's like about her coffee. She wasn't happy with the one Livia made for her, but I explained she doesn't know what she's doing yet.'

He turns to me, a worrying gleam of fake concern in his cow eyes. 'Don't worry, your Italian classes start in a few days. We might let you back behind the counter if you really apply yourself.'

The only thing I want to apply is my fist to his face, but I choke out a laugh as if I find him funny rather than ... well ... completely and utterly hateful and obnoxious. It's bad enough that he's so comfortable here, so at ease, while I'm stumbling over words and worried about mistakes. Now he's making me look incompetent at the bar, too!

I'm almost afraid to look at Nina, to see what a disappointment I am to her. But she's staring off into space as if caught in a memory. 'Signora Pedretti ... of course.' I think she's frowning, but it's so hard to tell. Then it's gone and she's reaching for Giulio's hand. 'Yes ... well, at least you're there to help, *caro*. I hope you're paying yourself on time. Don't wait for me to get out of hospital. It might be weeks yet.'

I turn my gasp of shock into a small coughing fit. Did I hear that right? Giulio's paying himself? From the till? My eyes dart between them, searching for signs that this is some kind of joke. But there are none.

Did Nina break her head as well as her leg? I want to demand answers, but Giulio has a knack for turning my words against me. Instead, I put my head down and tuck into what should be the most delicious carbonara I've eaten in my life (sorry Pa!). But my head is so full of questions about Giulio and the bar that I can't even take pleasure in my flawless twirling technique.

By the time we leave the hospital, I'm fuming inside and trying very hard to hide it. Giulio's charmed Nina again, even while throwing me under the bus. But I'm not letting him distract me. I need to figure out what's going on with that letter and why he's so determined to keep things from Nina and Ma and me. I just hope I can find out before he does any more damage. One thing's for sure; it's going to take every ounce of patience I can muster.

9

To say I hadn't been looking forward to language classes would be an understatement, but after one whole week of non-stop Giulio, and a dismal Sunday lunch at the hospital with Ma, my face could really do with a break. My cheeks literally ache from switching expressions all the time; scowling at Giulio when Ma's eyes are on me, forcing a smile when they're not. Getting away from the pretence, even if it's just for a few hours, is a welcome escape.

I find the school as easily as Nina said I would, just across the road on the corner of the street, the entrance tucked around the side. It looks like any other apartment building, with its graffitied walls and mustard stucco, but there are no geraniums or bougainvillea spilling over the balconies, just a line of teenagers filing in through the main door. I fall in behind a group of exchange students with matching backpacks and wait for my turn at reception, asking myself why I silenced that annoying little Duolingo owl. Would I be more confident now if I'd completed the Italian course on the app? Proper Italian, and not just the hybrid I speak with Ma and Pa.

'Livia Nardelli?' The receptionist repeats my name back to me, like she's expecting me to tell her there's been some mistake. '*Italiano?*'

A wave of heat washes over me as I nod, resisting the urge to apologize and confess that, yeah, I have the name and look the part, but I'm a fraud. I'm the equivalent of a red-haired, freckle-faced Morag McDonald turning up to learn the chorus of 'Auld Lang Syne'.

The receptionist switches to English, clearly changing her opinion of me as she points at the stairwell. 'Second floor. First door on the right.'

Inside the classroom, the exchange students have already claimed one entire side of the U-shaped desk arrangement and are chatting together in a language I don't recognize. Posters of the Colosseum, the Spanish Steps and other famous landmarks adorn the walls and it's crazy to think they're nearby, beyond this street and these four walls. But I can just imagine what Giulio would say if I took a day off to go sightseeing. *Turista.*

'*Ehi!*'

I'm so lost in thought, it takes me a moment to realize the petite girl with the swingy ponytail is saying hello to me. I do the thing where I look over my shoulder then point awkwardly to myself, but she continues to nod and smile, revealing the whitest, wonkiest teeth I've ever seen.

I must be staring because she laughs, an even bigger grin splitting her face. 'I know, I know, the teeth are . . . a thing.' She holds out her hand. 'I'm Kenzi. I saw you arrive by yourself and I'm on my own too, so . . .'

I stutter an apology. I feel awful – it's like when people stare at my nose – but the truth is, it wasn't her teeth that caught me off guard, it was her words, spoken in perfect Italian. I may not be able to copy it, but I know a Roman accent when I hear one. Her vowels are open and lengthened, like Pa's, and the endings are dropped, too. I give her the same quizzical look the receptionist gave me. She's every bit the Italian teenager – stylishly casual, and a little bit sophisticated. But her name . . .

'I'm Moroccan,' she says, as if reading my thoughts. 'On paper, anyway. Where are you from?'

I must make a face because she quickly covers her mouth, though I don't think it's to hide her teeth – I've just met her, but she's already giving off Isla-vibes.

'Sorry,' she says. 'I hate it when people ask me that! And now I'm doing it.'

I shake my head. 'It's fine. Really.'

Normally, I hate that question too, but somehow I don't mind giving Kenzi the whole 'born in Scotland to Italian parents' spiel. And, anyway, I'm also curious about her. What's she doing here when she's clearly fluent — accent and all?

Before I can ask, a guy in mustard chinos and a creased T-shirt — creased as in you can see exactly where it was folded — walks into the room.

'*Salve a tutti!*' he announces, before hooking a thumb towards his chest. '*Io sono* Massimiliano.' Only he says it like this: I-o so-no Mas-si-mi-li-a-no, stretching out each syllable as if he's spelling it instead of saying it.

He looks and sounds like a kids' TV presenter, Inner Isla says.

I'd laugh, but there's an A-frame whiteboard with the numbers one to ten in Italian on it. Am I in the wrong class? Or worse, did Nina and Giulio put me in with the beginners? But Kenzi's here, I remind myself. Then Mas-si-mi-li-a-no explains, through a combination of melodrama and mime, that the teacher for the Intermediate to Advanced class had a fa-mi-ly e-mer-gen-cy — big sad face — and so he'll be teaching both classes together — wild hand circling. He doesn't know for how long — points to an imaginary watch and shrugs.

'*Aiuto*. It's like charades . . . but you're allowed to speak Italian,' I whisper to Kenzi, sinking into my seat.

She does her own mime of someone looking supremely bored and we smother a shared laugh.

I check how everyone else is reacting to Mas-si-mi-li-a-no, and see a mix of genuine interest, mild concern and abject horror on the twenty or so faces around me. I'm pretty sure I've just identified the beginners, intermediates and advanced students based on that alone.

One boy in a graphic tee and cargo shorts is actually clutching his head, his silky black hair spiking up through his fingers.

We spend a painful hour going around the class making introductions, and another working on photocopies of the numbers one to ten. Just when I'm sure I won't be coming back, no matter how ungrateful I seem to Nina, we're shuffled into small groups and I find myself sitting in a four with Kenzi, Graphic Tee Boy, who introduces himself as Ren, and Sofia, a Brazilian girl with a bright yellow mane of hair – yellow yellow, not blonde-gone-wrong yellow.

We start with the usual 'how many brothers and sisters do you have?' questions, but by the end of the lesson, the four of us are actually having a conversation.

Ren, who's here to do a crash course before he

starts culinary school in September, describes himself as a matcha crème brûlée – his way of saying he's half Japanese, half French, and obsessed with fusion cuisine. Then, for an uncomfortable minute, I wonder if I'm a deep-fried pizza. Yeah, not quite the same thing.

Sofia, unlike Mas-si-mi-li-a-no, talks at 100 kilometres an hour, although I suspect it's so we don't notice there's some Portuguese thrown in. I love how she just goes for it, though – guessing at words and making them up as she goes along. We don't catch everything, but the languages must have something in common because, between us, we piece together quite a bit. Her Italian grandfather emigrated to Brazil from Bologna when he was young, and she gets Italian mixed up with Bolognese dialect. A year older than us, she's technically on a gap year to 'explore her roots', but she's also putting off telling her parents university's not for her. She tells us this while answering the notifications popping up on her multiple social media feeds at the same time.

I'm actually smiling by the time we leave the classroom. It's a little safe space where I can practise Italian without Nina staring down her Roman nose at me, the bar customers looking nervous, or Giulio waiting for me to slip up like I did with Signora Pedretti's *caffè*.

Ren and Sofia peel off towards the Metro as soon as we're out in the street, but Kenzi falls into step beside me.

'That's my nonna's bar.' My arms are wrapped around our new workbooks, so I tilt my chin towards it instead.

'This one?' Kenzi considers it as if it were a painting and I clutch the books more tightly, seeing it through her eyes – the tired old furniture, the dim lighting, the two elderly men playing cards outside. A couple of girls hover in the doorway. For a second, it looks like they're going to go in but, after a whispered exchange, they move off again, probably to the livelier bars down the street where young people are clinking their brightly coloured *aperitivi*, laughing and chatting before going to dinner.

'*Carino*,' Kenzi says at last.

I wrinkle my nose. *Cute?* Does she mean Giulio? He's sitting inside, bent over a textbook, completely oblivious. My face heats up at the thought, but Kenzi gestures to the outdoor tables and I realize she's talking about the bar, not him, which makes me feel strangely relieved.

'It's nice that there are still places like this where older people aren't pushed out. I could see my jad – that's my mama's father – coming here, if he ever went out. Not that he does ... or will,' she says, rolling her eyes.

I pause at Kenzi's words. Where would the regulars go if Nina's bar weren't around? Ma and Pa have been chatting non-stop about its finances on their nightly catch-ups. And I've seen enough to know breakfast is the only time it's actually busy. The worry gnaws at me, especially with Giulio so easily slipping behind the counter as if he owns the place – could he be dipping into the profits too?

10

'Let me guess, two cappuccinos, right?' Giulio scoffs as I walk past his table to get Kenzi and me something to drink – he thinks we're both so cluelessly foreign we have no idea it's practically against the law to drink cappuccinos after 11 a.m. here.

Inner Isla rears her devious head. *Smile, Liv. Flies prefer honey, remember?*

I force my lips to curve upwards. But pretending to find Giulio funny is like swallowing an entire barrel of vinegar.

My heart sinks when he gets up and leans over the counter, eyeing me as I pour two small bottles of lemony *cedrata* into glasses filled with ice. 'Hope you're paying for that, Scotland. You're supposed to be helping Nina, not guzzling her profits, remember?'

'Don't worry, Ma's on it with the takings.' My eyes slide to where she's tucked into a corner with a calculator, rifling through a box file like she's lost something. She's so focused, she hasn't even noticed I'm back from Italian class.

Giulio goes still, his cow eyes holding mine for a beat longer than they should. Is he worried Ma knows something? Or I do? I plaster on another syrupy smile and grab our drinks as he rushes back to his table. He's stuffing his textbook into his backpack when I pass and, for a second, I think I spot the edge of a bank statement, similar to the ones in Ma's file, sticking out from between the pages.

He follows me outside and starts talking to Kenzi the way some people speak to Ma and Pa in Scotland – the way some customers speak to me. Loud and slow, like she's stupid.

'How. Was. Your. Lesson?'

Kenzi raises an eyebrow, unimpressed, and I grin as she points to Giulio's table and fires back in perfect Italian, 'Hey, I recognize that textbook you were looking at. What *liceo* do you go to?'

His head jerks back in surprise. 'Ehm . . . I go to Liceo Visconti. It's just off—'

'I know where it is,' Kenzi interrupts. 'I've heard they have an excellent Latin programme.'

I smirk as Giulio's face cycles through a host of emotions – confusion, suspicion, embarrassment and finally, a grudging admiration. He runs a hand through his hair, which, annoyingly, falls back into its perfect mussed-up style. 'So you met Livia at Italian class? Isn't that . . . too easy for you?'

I flap my hands at Kenzi behind Giulio's back, silently begging her not to spill the beans about our mind-numbingly basic Italian class. I can just see Giulio's smug grin if he finds out I've spent three hours saying '*Ciao, come ti chiami?*' while he's been conjugating verbs in Latin.

Kenzi gives me the slightest of nods. 'Oh, it's a new experimental programme. We'll be looking at various dialects across Italy.' She leans back in her chair; her feet, encased in chunky fisherman sandals that would look frumpy on me, are planted wide apart, giving her a confident air.

I bite my lip to keep from laughing as Giulio's eyelid twitches. 'I signed Livia up myself and it was definitely language lessons.'

Kenzi waves her hand. 'It's a free upgrade for those of us who aced the placement test they gave us at the beginning of the lesson.'

I swallow a smile. Even I'm half convinced by Kenzi's quickly concocted lies.

'Right, well . . .' He rocks back on his heels. 'I'd better get back. Some of us have work to do.'

I hold it together until he's out of earshot, stifling my laughter behind my hand. 'Where did that come from?'

Kenzi shrugs. 'Trust me, when you've got an older brother who's always trying to ruin your fun, you get good at lying. What's the deal with you two anyway?'

I give her the lowdown on Giulio, surprised at how easily the words come. I'm not even self-conscious about my accent, like I am when I speak to Nina and Giulio, though I know I'm making a few mistakes.

'So . . . why *are* you taking classes?' I ask when I finish. I've been dying to know all afternoon, but we ran out of time during our little group chat.

Kenzi swirls the ice cubes in her drink with her straw. 'It's a blood thing.'

NOT the answer I was expecting. She must see this because she leans forward, like Isla does when she's sharing a secret.

'You've got Italian parents, right?'

I nod.

'And Sofia's got an Italian nonno, *sì*?'

I nod again.

'Well, I don't have any Italian relatives, so I'm not entitled to Italian citizenship, even though I was born here and have never been to Morocco in my life . . . or any other country for that matter.'

My mouth falls open. 'What?'

'I can apply to be Italian when I'm eighteen. My

brother's going through the process now.' She pauses to sip her drink. 'He's the one who convinced my parents that having a language certificate will boost my application. Even if it's just from a summer intensive.'

My knee bounces under the table, irritated on her behalf — and my own. Technically, I'm entitled to an Italian passport, but Ma and Pa have never bothered applying for one. Maybe they don't see me as truly Italian, not in the way they are. But would it even matter? My British passport doesn't make me feel British, and Kenzi's is from a country she's never even set foot in.

'Does it bother you?' I ask. 'Having to come to class?'

'It did . . . until Mama told my brother he'd have to babysit our little sister while I'm there.' She flashes a toothy grin. 'That'll teach him to interfere.'

I sip my own drink, savouring the sugary citrus tang. Then another question pops up in my head. 'So . . . do you speak Arabic, then?'

Kenzi makes a so-so gesture with her hand. 'We speak it at home, but Italian's my first language.'

I sigh. 'I bet your Moroccan accent isn't as bad as my Italian one.'

'Ha! Just ask my—'

But before Kenzi finishes her reply, one of the men

playing cards leans back in his chair and asks, 'Did you say you speak Arabic?' His question makes Kenzi stiffen, but then he adds, 'Do you write it, too?'

Kenzi nods but doesn't say anything as the man hands her a crumpled note from his wallet.

'Could you write "one tablet, three times a day after meals" here, and "once a day on an empty stomach" here?'

Kenzi pulls a pen from her bag and chews thoughtfully on the cap as she writes. 'I think that's it,' she says, handing back the paper.

'*Grazie.* You've been very helpful.' The man taps her hand gently with the folded note before going back to his card game.

'What was that about?' I whisper, leaning in.

Kenzi sighs. 'Looks like he's trying to help someone. Lots of immigrants rely on other people to translate prescriptions and stuff, especially us second-generation kids. It's a whole thing.'

I nod. Before Isla became one of the family, she found it strange that Ma and Pa would call me from my room to make phone calls for them, or that I'm the one who speaks to the waiters when we eat out. The day before we came to Rome, I helped Pa fill out a form to renew his driver's licence. Stuff like that is second nature to me. And I realize there's more to straddling two cultures than getting an accent right or drinking cappuccinos at the right time of day – teenagers like Kenzi and me are like bridges between two places, with a foot on either side.

11

The arrival of a voice note from Isla wakes me at 6.47 a.m. I sit up, heart pounding, instantly wide awake – Edinburgh's an hour behind. Why is she messaging me so early?

'*Any dirt on Giuli-hot?*'

I sigh with relief as her teasing tone floats out of the speaker. Right. Not an emergency then.

I'm still shaking my head when I pass Nina's room on my way to the kitchen. Ma's sprawled out in the middle of the bed in her vest and knickers, half-hugging the ever-present box file that's spilling paperwork on to the mattress beside her. The horror of it propels me straight to the fridge where I stashed a leftover *bombolone alla crema* before I went to bed last night. I can't think of a better breakfast than a custard doughnut with an Italian upgrade. There's also a slice of *pizza bianca* stuffed with wafer-thin slices of mortadella that I've earmarked for my morning snack.

Grabbing a small carton of apricot juice, I head up to the roof terrace and the promise of a breathtaking view. I'm not disappointed. The sky is streaked with wisps of pink and orange, brightening even as I look at it. It must be seven on the dot because bells start tolling all around me, and I remember Ma telling me there are over nine hundred churches around this city. I seek out a few domes and bell towers, finding them easily.

Not trusting my ability to get into the hammock with my breakfast in one hand and phone in the other, I perch on the stone balustrade; the red-tiled roof sticking out directly below it giving me the illusion of safety. I FaceTime Isla to discuss messaging etiquette and how NOT to give me a heart attack first thing in the morning.

I almost think I've called the wrong person when her make-up-free face appears on the screen. '*Ommioddio*, you're spending so much time at the cattery – you're turning into Ma. What are you doing up so early?'

She sticks her tongue out at me before stretching her mouth into a gigantic yawn. 'Emergency cat drop-off in half an hour. Your dad had to leave super early for a wedding up north, so your mum said she'd pay me extra if I came in for six.' She rubs her fingers together in the universal gesture for money. 'I'm going to have my helix pierced by the time we go back to school.' She yawns again, then squints at the screen. 'Are you . . . outside already?'

Instead of answering, I pan the phone camera around the rooftop. I can't see her face, but her gasp of awe is even louder than the hum of scooters and the clatter of bins being emptied down below.

'You'd better bring me with you next time, or else,' she threatens, as I show her the view from the other side before flipping the phone back to me.

'So . . . how's it going with Giulio?'

'A-ma-zing,' I blurt, my words overlapping with her question as I take my first bite of the soft, doughy *bombolone*.

'Really? You've changed your tune.'

I stick my own tongue out. 'Ha ha. Very funny. I meant this.' I hold my breakfast up to the camera. 'Way tastier, trust me.'

'Aw, shame. I've got a bet on with your mum that your first French kiss is going to be Italian . . . she thinks the same though, so we can't work out how to decide the winner.'

'Right, that's it!' I splutter. 'No more unsupervised calls between you and Ma.'

A door creaks open behind me and I snap my head around. Giulio's on his roof terrace just a few paces away . . . definitely within hearing range of this super-embarrassing conversation.

Isla's hazel eyes fill the screen. 'Hey! What's up? You've gone bright red!'

'Call you later!' I close her down before she says anything else and study Giulio's face. How much did he hear? I squirm inside at the thought of him knowing I've never properly kissed a boy before. Not unless you count the school Christmas dance when a boy in the year above me leant in and half-mashed his lips against mine before running off to the boys' toilets. It's . . . too private. Something I'll have to remind Ma about. Honestly, the sooner that woman's back with her cats, the better.

'*Buongiorno.*' Giulio links his hands behind his neck and stretches, his T-shirt hitching above the waist of his jeans with the movement. My eyes snag on a stripe of tanned abs.

'Enjoying the view?' he adds, his sly grin telling me he doesn't mean the cityscape.

A blush crawls over my skin. A hangover from my conversation with Isla, I tell myself. Because I'm definitely not falling for Giulio's charms like some tourist girl – not when there's so much about him I don't trust.

'It was better before you showed up,' I reply, reaching for a jokey comment to disguise my next question.

'What are you doing here anyway? Making calls?'

Giulio freezes, arms still clasped at the nape of his neck, and I wonder if I've given myself away. Scrabbling for an excuse, I show him my own phone. 'The reception's much better up here, isn't it?'

His arms drop to his sides and he leans one hip against the railing separating his roof terrace from Nina's. 'I just like to come up here before the day begins. It's peaceful.'

He sounds sincere and, for a moment, he's less like the cocky barista and more like . . . well, a real person.

'Yeah, it is nice,' I admit, admiring the view – Rome's famous landmarks tantalizingly within reach.

When I turn back, Giulio's watching me with an odd expression.

'What?' I ask defensively.

He shakes his head slightly. 'Nothing. Just . . . you look different when you're not making weird faces at me.'

I open my mouth to protest, but he's already turning away. As he disappears back inside, I'm left feeling . . . restless. I finish my *bombolone* with less enthusiasm than before, wiping my sugary fingers on my pyjama shorts. The peaceful mood from earlier has vanished.

My phone pings again as I get up to leave. It's

another message from Isla:

Having a little rooftop rendezvous with Giulio, are we?

I send a selfie of my unimpressed face – a face that is entirely alone on the terrace – ignoring the lingering warmth in my cheeks.

Ma's rinsing a chopping board in the kitchen when I go downstairs. Her tortoiseshell hair is tangled and matted on one side, but at least she's spared my eyeballs further trauma and thrown on a long T-shirt.

'Ah, *eccoti*. I thought I heard you up there. Were you on the phone?'

'Yeah, just Isla,' I say, grabbing a glass of water. 'She was at the cattery in time for that emergency drop-off, by the way.'

I want to bring up their stupid bet, but I don't want to open up a kissing conversation with Ma either – a can of worms, if ever there was one.

'You're looking a bit flushed, *tesoro*. Everything OK?'

'I'm fine,' I say quickly. 'Just . . . the sun. It's already getting warm out there.'

Ma crosses to the fridge and starts pulling out peaches, apricots, kiwis and melons – all so much brighter and juicier than what I'm used to. 'Give me a hand with these? I'm making a *macedonia* for the bar.'

I nod – mouth already watering; I love fruit salad – and look for a tea towel to dry off the chopping board. I find one in the drawers beneath the kitchen window; a window that looks directly on to the building next door. When I look up a bit, I realize it also offers quite a good view of Giulio's roof terrace.

A sinking feeling settles in my stomach as I catch Ma's reflection in the glass – and the infuriatingly knowing smile on her face.

Did she see Giulio up there? Did she hear our conversation?

My mind races. I've got to be more careful. The last thing I need is Ma thinking she has actual evidence of me being the cliché foreign girl. But at the same time, that brief exchange on the terrace felt like a little breakthrough; like I might actually be capable of pulling off this whole friends charade.

I start chopping, taking my frustrations out on a jumbo watermelon. The quicker I get closer to Giulio and find out what he's up to, the better.

12

I offer to open up the bar while Ma has a shower, and my heart rate kicks up a notch at being alone and in charge for the first time. Only the low hum of the refrigerators and the clatter of a rolling shutter cranking up next door keeps me company. I flick the switch on the coffee machine, half-expecting it to blow up in my face, but it hisses and gurgles in the usual way and I let out a shaky breath.

Then, something unexpected catches my eye – a sleek, modern-looking air-conditioning unit installed near the ceiling. I can't believe I missed it; it's so glaringly out of place. But maybe the promise of cool air will entice more customers. I find a remote control attached to a little plastic holder on the wall beneath it. A silent, cool breeze blows out of the vents and I mentally pat myself on the back. Surely Giulio should have thought about doing this?

With a new bounce in my step, I secure the door shutters to their hooks on the outside wall and find a white box with the logo of a local *pasticceria* on one of the outdoor tables. The underside of the thin cardboard is still warm when I pick it up, the pastries fresh out of the oven and fragrant. I know I've just had a *bombolone*, but ...

'*Buongiorno.*'

I'm barely back behind the counter when the first customer of the day walks in. He's wearing the unofficial uniform of retired Italian men: beige trousers, polo shirt, newspaper under one arm, and bushy white eyebrows in a tanned face. At first, I think he's just another regular – it's hard to tell them apart – but his distinctive sideburns mark him as the man who asked Kenzi to translate that prescription. He's squinting at me, though I can't say if he recognizes me – teenagers must be just as interchangeable to him – or if he's wondering what I'm doing behind the counter. Maybe both.

He chooses a corner table next to the tall metal stand displaying crisps and snacks, and calls out his order. '*Un caffè e un cornetto, per favore.*'

Phew. Coffee and croissant. Couldn't be simpler.
'*Sì, certo. Un momento solo.*'

Cavolo, I should've stuck with a one-word answer, because he pauses in the act of opening his newspaper, his brows pulling together in one long fuzzy line. I try not to let it knock my confidence. I can't get such a simple order wrong, can I?

I'm still asking myself that question when I open the *pasticceria* box and find at least eight different types of *cornetto*, none of them labelled. The Nutella ones are oozing clues, as are the ones filled with berry jam . . . but the others? They're sitting there, pretending to have no filling at all. My hand hovers over the crescent-shaped pastries like I'm defusing a bomb but don't know which wire to cut. Sugar glaze? Sugar crystals? Egg wash? I decide to keep it simple and go for one that has no finish at all.

I'm just taking it over, pretending I haven't had a mini meltdown over a box of pastries, when Giulio comes into the bar, looking surprised to find it already open.

I'm about to give him a smug smirk of my own – look at me, managing all by myself – when the man clears his throat.

'*Signorina?* This is not my usual *cornetto.*'

Giulio peers at the pastry, then whisks it away and swaps it for a puffier one with an egg wash. 'You'll have to forgive our new barista, Enrico,' he explains in a stage whisper. 'She's Scottish.'

'Ahhh!' Enrico's eyes light up. 'My wife and I spent our honeymoon there. Beautiful country.' He bites into his pastry with a satisfied nod before adding,

'Terrible weather.'

I wait for Giulio to point out that I can't even get the classic Italian breakfast right, but instead he joins me behind the bar. 'Enrico's a bit resistant to change,' he whispers. 'The *cornetto* you gave him was vegan. Easy mistake to make, Scotland.'

'Err . . . Thanks?' I look at his face but, strangely, I don't detect any smirk or sarcasm. Is it possible our brief encounter on the roof terrace shifted something between us? Even that stupid nickname he keeps using doesn't carry its usual sting.

Ma bumps the connecting door open with her backside, hands holding the huge bowl of fruit salad waiting to be portioned out. She's wearing jeans and a simple cotton blouse that's buttoned up slightly wrong, but it's still a big improvement on the cat-hair joggers and T-shirt she usually wears. '*Buongiorno*, you two . . . at it already, eh?'

I go deathly still, all too aware of what this scene must look like through Ma's boyfriend-obsessed eyes – like I'm flustered by Giulio rather than another customer mishap.

'If you mean already working, then yes, I am . . . but Giulio?' I shoot him a cold glance, making sure Ma sees it too. 'Shouldn't you be setting up outside?'

Giulio gives me a mock salute. '*Subito*, Livia.'

I ignore the sharp twinge in my stomach as he goes to open up the sun umbrellas, and that I've gone back to being Livia and not Scotland. It's not like I want us to be actual friends, I remind myself. And being nice to him hasn't got me any closer to finding out what he's up to anyway. But I still don't feel as triumphant as I'd like to.

Enrico clears his throat loudly and I hurry to make his coffee, but as I set it in front of him, I notice he's rubbing his neck, his teeth clenched in a grimace as he glares at the air-conditioning unit.

'Oh!' Ma must have been watching our exchange because she steps in, looking up in confusion. '*Chiedo scusa*, that's not supposed to be on.' She makes a big deal of switching off the air conditioning and reassuring Enrico it will stay off.

He smiles, relieved, stretching his neck from side to side.

Ma grasps my elbow and steers me away from his table. 'You'll have the regulars coming in with neck braces if you switch that thing on.'

I shrink into myself, hating that she knows it was me . . . that it didn't cross her mind for a second that Giulio might make a rookie error like that.

She strokes my cheek, finishing with a pat. '*Scusami, tesoro*. It's just . . . air conditioning is a big thing here. The older generation think it can make them ill . . . or give them a stiff neck. We can't afford to lose any customers.' Her eyes shine with sympathy and concern, but whether the concern is for me or the damage I'm doing to Nina's business is less clear.

Giulio collects Enrico's empty plate and cup and I hear them chatting and joking together. 'It's too hot for her here, she's trying to feel more at home.'

The knot in my stomach tightens. Giulio thinks he's so perfect, smoothing over the ripples I create with his confident charm. But Ma will soon see I'm not the only one slipping up. Forget waiting until I have proof, it's time to tell her everything he's been doing behind her back.

13

'*Buongiorno a tutti!*'

I've been unsuccessfully trying to get Ma on her own when Signora Pedretti swoops into the bar in that sudden, unsettling way of hers – a tall, glossy teenage girl at her heels. '*Due caffè, per favore*, Giulio. And make them perfect. I've been telling Flaminia here that you're the best barista in Rome.'

'No pressure, then.' Unflustered by the tall order that would have sent me into a panic, Giulio busies himself with the coffee machine while I study the new arrival.

Signora Pedretti's mentioned this girl before – the god-daughter whose friends are away all summer, like Giulio's. Her hair is a colour Italians would call blonde, but my friends in Scotland would say is light brown. And her nose – it's so small I bet her oversized sunglasses are perched on her head because they'd just slide right off her face.

'And this,' Signora Pedretti says, gesturing towards me, 'is Livia. She lives in Scotland, but she speaks

Italian. She has the most adorable little accent. Go on, Livia, say something.'

My face ignites as all eyes turn to me.

Flaminia smiles sympathetically. 'She says that about me too, Livia – just because I live on the other side of the city.'

I don't believe her for a second, but I'm grateful when everyone laughs and the attention shifts away from me. I like this girl. She's beautiful *and* nice.

'So, what are you two ladies up to today?' Giulio places the coffees on the counter, earning a pleased hum from Signora Pedretti. She raises her cup and inhales deeply before answering.

'Flaminia is helping me shop for a new phone; I'm being bullied into getting one with the Google on it. Some bureaucratic nonsense with my pension means I need to be inline.'

'Online. It's online.' Flaminia looks pained, as though she's bracing for a long day of correcting her godmother.

Signora Pedretti winks at Giulio. 'Perhaps you should come, *caro*? I'm sure Flaminia would love to have another young person around.'

Flaminia's cheeks flush the perfect shade of pink, her blush more like carefully applied make-up than the blotchy mess I turn into.

Is Signora Pedretti playing matchmaker?

A strange knot forms in my stomach but, before I can examine the feeling, Signora Pedretti lays a hand on Ma's forearm. 'Can we have a word, *cara*?'

Ma's eyes flick to me for a second. 'Of course . . . but let's go outside.'

What now? I sigh as they step out into the street, leaving me with yet another mystery to unravel – right alongside Giulio's letter-thieving, secretive calls and snooping.

'So, phone shopping with Signora Pedretti? You're brave!' Giulio presses his lips together like he's trying not to laugh.

Flaminia groans. 'Don't! I'm already dreading the sales spiel. She just needs something basic and user-friendly, but they'll probably try to sell her something ridiculous.'

He reaches for a pad next to the till, ripping off a page and scribbling something on it. He hands it to Flaminia. 'Try this place – the guy who owns it is my friend's dad. Tell him I sent you.' He pauses, then adds, 'Hang on.' He scribbles again. 'That's my number too, in case you need help.'

I feel like a third wheel. And I can't help noticing how nice and friendly Giulio is when he's talking to anyone but me. The knot in my stomach twists tighter, but I push it down. I should be glad. Maybe they'll hit it off and Giulio will finally get out of my hair. Which is exactly what I want. Obviously.

Inner Isla facepalms so hard, I almost feel it myself.

Luckily, Ma and Signora Pedretti's little tête-à-tête doesn't last long, though it has an effect long after Signora Pedretti disappears. Ma's distracted, looking surprised when Giulio calls out a coffee order, as if she's forgotten where she is or what she's doing. And stranger still, she tells Giulio and me that she's going to do Nina's lunch run today, even though it isn't Sunday and she was there just a few days ago.

I watch her face as she sets the coffee grinder in motion, scanning for any insight into what's going on, but it's hard to think straight over the deafening whine of coffee beans being blitzed.

When the grinder finally stops, Ma turns to Giulio. 'OK if I take your Vespa?'

His shoulders tense and his eyes drop to his hi-tops.

I'm lost for words too. Ma? On a Vespa?

'*Ehm, va bene,*' Giulio finally murmurs, though he looks like the words are being pulled from his mouth against his will.

'It was your nonna's, right?' Ma says, surprising us both. 'Your mamma and I used to ride it to the beach when we were teenagers.' She tuts when I fail to hold back a snort. 'Yes, we were your age too, once upon a time.'

'... a long, long time ago,' I mutter.

Ma continues talking to Giulio. 'Francesca's at the sea now, isn't she? Will she be back soon?'

I pretend to be fascinated by a scratch on the counter but, if I had whiskers, they'd be twitching like mad as I listen for his response. I've been wondering if Giulio even has parents, given his intense need to worm his way into Nina's life.

He kicks the toe of his trainer against the rubber seal of the fridge under the counter. 'The parents she nannies for need her all summer. She said she'll try to visit, though.' His long cow-lashes are lowered.

Ma grimaces. 'What about your papà? Is he still driving lorries?'

Laughter echoes from the street outside, and Giulio's head shoots up as if he's hoping there are customers to be looked after. 'He's on his way to Turkey, but might be back for a couple of days in August...'

This gives me pause. I mean Pa's away a lot in the spring and summer, but Ma's always around – even if she's too busy pandering to her kitty clients and their fussy owners to pay too much attention to me. But not having either parent? I can't imagine it.

'That must be tough, Giulio,' Ma says, as if reading my thoughts. 'On you and your parents. They must hate being apart.'

Giulio snorts, then tries to cover it up with a cough. 'I'll . . . ehm . . . get you the spare helmet.'

I get a weird feeling in my stomach as I watch him leave, like a pang of sympathy I'd rather not feel – not for Giulio, anyway.

14

I prop myself in the doorway as Ma eases herself on to the saddle of the Vespa – a saddle she gets entirely to herself. I push away the memory of how tricky it's been sharing that tiny space with Giulio on our daily hospital visits – clinging to him as we bump over potholes and uneven streets paved in *sampietrini*, the cube-shaped cobbles that are so distinctly Roman.

She turns the key in the ignition and revs the handle, and I can't help being secretly impressed. I even sneak a quick video of her driving off and send it to Pa.

He replies immediately.

Bellissima! A real classic. The Vespa's not bad either . . .

I groan at his reply – and the winky face at the end of his message – but I shouldn't complain after what Giulio (reluctantly) shared earlier. I might cover my ears when they blow kisses to each other on their nightly calls . . . but it's sweet, really. Not that I would EVER admit it to their faces.

The bar is quiet for a while after that, so I'm able to keep a close eye on Giulio. He spends most of his time by the till, either peering into the street as if he's looking out for his precious Vespa, or on his phone.

I watch his fingers flying over the screen in bursts as if he's messaging back and forth. A weird prickly feeling takes hold: is it Flaminia messaging for advice? But then another thought edges in – what if it's the same person he was talking to on the rooftop? The one who sent that letter?

'So . . .' I run a cloth along the countertop, my tone casual. 'Who's that you're messaging?'

'Wouldn't you like to know?' Giulio doesn't even glance up as a new message pops on to his screen, but his soft chuckle indicates it's not the person from the roof. I tell myself I'm disappointed because I'd wanted to catch him red-handed . . . but I'm not entirely sure that's true.

I'm grateful for the distraction when an elderly couple come in for a *panino al prosciutto* and a cappuccino – even if it does prompt Giulio to flash me one of his teasing smirk-smiles and say, 'You're up, Scotland. Go and serve your people.'

I roll my eyes out of habit, but his comment – though clearly a dig at how only tourists would ask for that particular food and drink combo – doesn't annoy me like it would have on day one. Maybe Isla's on to something with this 'pretend friends' thing. It's definitely giving me an extra layer of protection against his little jabs.

I make the cappuccinos next and even attempt a simple leaf shape with the steamed milk, following the steps of the video I saw online. But it comes out more blobby than botanical. And, of course, Giulio has abandoned his phone and is now watching my botched attempt at coffee art.

'You might want to master the basics first, Scotland. The froth should be creamy, not foamy.'

I grit my teeth and try again, determined not to let him get to me. But as he leans in to show me the 'correct' way to steam milk, the warmth of his breath near my ear makes me fumble the jug. The jet of hot steam scorches the back of my hand and I yelp.

Giulio reacts instantly, gently grabbing my wrist and guiding my hand under the cold-water tap. His touch is confusing – firm, yet kind. I'm left both grateful and irritated because, if he'd just minded his own business, I wouldn't have burnt myself in the first place.

Triggered by her boy-proximity radar, Ma comes back from her lunch run to find Giulio and me with our heads together at the sink.

'I had an accident with the steamer, OK?' I know I sound defensive, but I wish she wouldn't keep looking at us like that. I pull my hand away from Giulio, as if his touch is another kind of burn, and show Ma the red streak developing below my knuckles.

She switches to concerned mode. '*Aspetta*. I saw some aloe vera upstairs.'

She returns with a small, crumpled tube and gently dabs the cool, soothing gel on to the back of my hand. Her head is bent to the task and I notice the circles under her eyes are darker than usual. Her eyelids are red too, as if she's been rubbing them . . . or crying?

'How was lunch?' I ask, trying to gauge her mood.

She hesitates before answering, her voice soft. 'You don't have to work in the bar, you know. I hadn't realized business was this slow. You should be out seeing the sights. Giulio and I can manage without you.'

Turista. I draw in a sharp breath.

'Oops, sorry, did I hurt you?'

She did, but not in the way she thinks. It hurts more knowing Ma sees me as a tourist in my own family rather than someone who belongs behind this bar.

Giulio's attention splits between us and the street outside, and when he hurries out I think he's trying to intercept the post again. But then I see a man loitering near his precious Vespa, motioning to the bike. People are always stopping to admire it, although they're usually tourists, and this man looks nothing like one.

Still, I'm glad Giulio can't hear me when I say, 'I want to help, to properly be a part of this.'

Ma caps the tube of aloe vera, and sighs. 'I know, *tesoro*. But . . . it's Rome! You could see—'

'I'm not here as a *turista*, OK? And this is Rome too, isn't it?' I gesture around the bar, my voice loud even to my own ears. I want to say more – say it louder still – but . . . how can Ma possibly understand? She knows exactly where she comes from, where she belongs. I turn away and run to the connecting door, my throat thick with brewing tears . . . because if I don't belong here, where do I belong?

15

I kick off my shoes and head straight up to the roof terrace, wiping my cheeks as I go. The sun is directly above me in a cloudless blue sky, the concrete beneath my feet as hot as the jet of steam that burnt my hand. My quiet sniffles turn to sobs as I dash over to the hammock and pour myself into the stripy fabric with even less grace than the last time. The sun-warmed cotton embraces me like a hug, taking the weight of my body. But it doesn't lift my mood.

I was so sure I'd find a sense of belonging here, in the city and the business where my family's roots are buried deep, but I keep getting things wrong – the wrong coffee, the wrong pastry, even the wrong air temperature. Why is everything so difficult here? Why can't I just . . . fit? The city's noise, the distant hum of traffic and the bursts of calls and chatter from the streets below, all feel like a world away – someone else's world.

I shift on to my side, trying to shake off my

thoughts, and my phone digs into my hip. I don't reach for it. What's the point? Isla's too far away to help, and what would I even say? That I'm homesick – for a home I don't have?

I close my eyes, wishing my brain had an off switch.

That's when I hear the scuff of footsteps again. I wriggle up a bit and peer over the side of the hammock to see Giulio appear on the other terrace. Why is he always turning up when I'm here, too? Is he trying to annoy me?

I duck out of sight, but it's too late. The dull clank of metal tells me he's climbing over the railing. His long shadow falls over my body as he leans his forearms on the balustrade beside me and stares down into the street below.

I roll my eyes, already guessing what's captured his attention. 'What is it with you and that Vespa? Are you so *fissato*, you have to watch it 24/7?'

Fissato. Obsessed. I didn't even know I knew that word. But it just came out. Naturally. Maybe I'm not as hopeless as Ma thinks I am.

Giulio's broad shoulders curve inwards. 'Yeah, well, I might not have it for much longer.'

I sit up slightly. Was I right? Does he need money to fix it? Then another thought occurs to me. 'Didn't it belong to your nonna?'

'Yes, but . . .' His head drops as if holding it up is too much effort, and it's clear we're both having a moment, each of us struggling with our own difficult thoughts. He sighs and stands up straight, his gaze snagging on the hand I'm cradling against my chest. 'You won't want to hear it anyway.'

'Try me . . .' And I'm surprised to realize I actually want to know.

He leans his back against the balustrade, considering me for a moment with those dark cow eyes. 'You hate that I'm close to Nina . . .'

I open my mouth to protest, but he nudges the hammock with his knee, making me swing precariously. 'Don't bother denying it. But she's been there for me, and . . .' He hesitates, then takes a deep breath. 'When my parents couldn't afford their own place, they moved into the two-bedroom apartment with my nonna – where I live now. But I had my own bedroom at Nina's because she wouldn't hear of me sleeping on the sofa when she had a spare room. So I used to move between the apartments via the roof terraces.'

'I didn't know that.' I blink, taken aback, although it explains why his stuff is in my room.

He shrugs, but I catch a glimpse of something

deeper. 'It wasn't always easy, you know? Being around my parents . . . they argued a lot. Nina's place was . . . a refuge.'

His jaw tightens as he speaks. It's clear he's not used to opening up like this. But I'm still confused. 'So . . . what does this have to do with your Vespa?'

A shutter falls over his face, the openness from a moment ago vanishing. 'Look, it's nothing for you to worry about. I only came out here to check on your hand. The burn . . . it was kind of my fault.'

My heart skips a beat at the unexpected concern. There's a softness in his voice that I hadn't noticed before, and it throws me off. 'It's fine,' I murmur, looking down at the red welt.

He nods, lashes lowered, masking his expression. 'Good.'

His phone buzzes, breaking the tension. He checks it quickly, his face hardening as he shoves it back into his pocket. 'Anyway . . .' Another forced smile. 'I need to go. Enjoy your . . . Italian dialect lessons.'

His lips twitch like he's suppressing a grin – a real one this time – telling me that, despite Kenzi's Oscar-worthy performance yesterday, he's still not buying it. I watch him disappear over to his own side of the roof.

The unease in my stomach deepens. There's definitely more going on with Giulio than he's letting on. Something involving the Vespa. Strangely, though, I'm curious not because I want to unmask Giulio, but simply because I want to know more about it . . . about him. As I settle back into the hammock, I realize something unexpected: a real friendship might be possible.

16

'*Ciao!*' I slide into my seat beside Kenzi, groaning at the topic of today's lesson written on the board. 'Food and drink, really?'

I've been coming here for a week now, but I'm learning more from my little asides with Kenzi than from anything we do in class.

Kenzi nudges me. 'Hey, you might pick up something useful for the bar ... Something that ... ahem ... might impress a certain someone?'

'*Uffa!* Not you, too.' I'm about to nudge her back, when I realize she's hit a nerve – though not about Giulio. '*Beh*, it's actually my mum I have to impress. She thought I was trying to kill off the oldies with the air conditioning the other day and now she wants me to go sightseeing instead.'

Kenzi snorts. 'Did she accuse you of being too Scottish?'

'Umm ... not in so many words.'

'My mama is not so subtle. Anytime my siblings and I do anything she disapproves of, we're either "too Italian" or "not Moroccan enough".' She uses a mimicking tone, and I assume it's supposed to be a Moroccan accent. 'That's multiple times a day, by the way.' Her face is a picture of long-suffering irritation.

My mood lightens. Kenzi and I might not share the same background, but we share the same struggles.

We fall silent when Mas-si-mi-li-a-no – who now insists we call him Mas-si – bounds to the front of the room. My muscles contract, bracing for his overenthusiastic greeting.

'*Ra-gaz-zi!*' he booms, circling the free-standing whiteboard like he's about to use it in a magic trick. 'Today, I am going to take you on a delicious journey!' He rubs a hand over his stomach for emphasis – as if he needs any.

Ren raises his hand. 'Would *baguetti* be a masculine or feminine noun?' he asks in his slightly wobbly Italian.

Mas-si frowns and smiles at the same time. 'Do you mean baguette or spaghetti?'

Ren chews on his lip like he's trying to taste the concept. 'A combination ... Not sure how, yet.'

Mas-si's grin dims by a couple of watts, as if he's unsure how to mime something that doesn't exist.

The lesson is, as expected, pretty basic, but Ren keeps it lively. He's such a foodie; he'd talk pasta varieties and regional dishes all day. It's interesting, though, listening to everyone speak with varying degrees of success. Kenzi could teach the class herself. Italian is her mother tongue, even if it isn't *her* mother's tongue. I'm surprised to realize I'm probably next, though I'm more comfortable speaking to Kenzi, Ren and Sofia than I am to Mas-si and the whole class. Sofia's got bags of confidence to mask her shaky Italian, and Ren ... well, he speaks the universal language of food.

We gather our things at the end of class and the four of us linger outside the main doors for a while, until Kenzi turns to me with a curious look. 'So, did you find out any more about Giulio's mysterious letter and phone call?'

'Ooh, *do que se trata?*' Sofia asks what's going on as she pushes her thick yellow hair behind her ears.

'Just the boy who's trying to steal my nonna, my summer job, and possibly my sanity.'

Sofia lifts one eyebrow. 'Tell me more ...'

'Why don't we come to the bar and help you spy on him?' Kenzi says.

Ren flings his arm around my shoulder. '*Bonne idée.* I would like a snack after today's lesson.'

'And I need a good coffee shot,' Sofia adds with a shrug.

At first, I think Sofia means she needs a shot of

coffee, but when we get to the bar – Ren still with an arm around my shoulders, as if he's weak with hunger – she orders a *ristretto* from a surly-looking Giulio, then spends a few minutes taking photos of it from different angles. 'For my travel blog,' she explains, not looking up.

I want to ask more, but I'm distracted by Giulio. He's scowling at Ren, who's just let me go to press his face against the refrigerated cabinet, pestering him about whether the *porchetta* filling comes from Ariccia, the nearby town famous for its roasted pork meat.

Ren finally settles on a huge slab of *pizza bianca* stuffed with lettuce and cured meats, and we're about to head outside when Sofia pulls me by the hem of my top to a table near the counter. 'Better view from here, *sim*?' she whispers in my ear.

Ren launches into his latest Franco-Japanese fusion ideas, wondering how to give them an Italian twist, when Enrico, who's seated at his usual table by the snack stand, clears his throat loudly. '*Scusa*,' he says, pausing to drape a fine-knit jumper around his shoulders when he recognizes me as the girl who tried to maim him with the A/C unit. 'Did you say French, Japanese and Italian cuisine together? My wife and I used to run a trattoria on this street, and I've never heard of such a thing.'

Ren's like a puppy with a waggly tail. '*Oui, monsieur!* I mean, *sì, signore*! I'm studying to become a chef, and I want to come up with my own signature style.'

Enrico beckons Ren over to his table. '*Interessante*. What kind of dishes do you make?'

They dive into a deep conversation about food, with Ren occasionally asking for help when his Italian fails him. Kenzi and I translate bits and pieces, while Sofia mostly nods along, keeping up with her latest posts. It's fascinating to hear Ren's schoolboy Italian mixing with Enrico's Roman expressions. But . . . they manage.

Giulio's still watching us from behind the counter – or rather, watching Ren – with an odd expression. Is he jealous Ren's just as good as he is at charming the local customers? I overhear Enrico saying he'd love to try onion and wasabi gyoza. So much for him not liking change.

'You've got good ideas, *ragazzo*,' Enrico says, getting to his feet. 'My wife would've liked you.'

'*Merci* . . . I mean, *grazie*!' Ren replies, puppy eyes bright and happy.

'Err . . . did you see that?' I ask Kenzi as Enrico shuffles out of the bar. 'Ren just picked up more Italian in that one conversation than all our lessons put together!'

'Amazing what a little real-world practice can do,' she murmurs. 'Mama and Baba didn't know a word of Italian when they moved here, but they picked it up soon enough. They had to.'

Like Ma and Pa, I think. Their English isn't fluent, but they can communicate well enough for their jobs. I wish I could spend more than one summer here – find out what it really means to be woven into the fabric of this city, instead of just a loose thread.

Kenzi wiggles in her seat. 'Actually, I've just had an idea. It's my English that needs improving. Why don't you and I do a language swap here after class? Give us both some real practice?'

I hesitate, remembering my vow not to speak a word of English this summer outside of my phone calls with Isla. But Kenzi's helped me with my Italian without even knowing it.

I smile. 'We could definitely do that.'

Ren nods enthusiastically, his hand resting on my shoulder for a moment. '*Moi aussi*, I want to talk about food in Italian *and* English. And I can bring snacks in exchange.'

Sofia, who's been quietly observing the bar, bites her lip. 'I would like to come too. But I do not know what to offer. I am good at social media ... or ...' Her voice drops, becoming suggestive. 'I could chat to

Giulio . . . find out more about him?'

I feel an unexpected twinge in my chest, as if the thought of Sofia liking Giulio is . . . uncomfortable. It's the same twinge I felt seeing him and Flaminia together. It's because Sofia and Flaminia are both so nice, I tell myself. And I don't want them falling for someone who can't be trusted.

17

In Scotland, storms have names. In Italy, heatwaves do. This one's called Caronte – after Charon, the boatman who ferries the dead to Hades. Accurate, because it's been slowly draining me since it swept in last night. Giulio and I are back on the lunch run and I'm peeling my shorts away from the backs of my thighs after our Vespa ride when I catch sight of myself in the little rear-view mirror attached to the handlebars. My hair has stayed in the shape of the helmet, clinging damply to my scalp in a round, frizzy mess, and my horrified expression says it all.

Giulio, of course, isn't wafting his shirt or tugging at his clothes. And because he bumped us over every pothole on the way here, to the point where I'm convinced he was doing it on purpose, I crashed into him so often I know he even smells good – a herby mix of mint and basil with a hint of the coffee roast we use at the bar. It's like he's been coated in some kind of heatproof spray. The sheer injustice of it must show on my face, or maybe he thinks I'm suffering from heatstroke, because he knocks his shoulder gently against mine and asks, 'You OK, Scotland?'

I speed-walk into the trattoria ahead of him so I don't have to fake-smile my way through his inevitable dig about me not being cut out to survive an Italian summer, but I'm suddenly face to face with the person behind the counter, waiting for me to order with a smile that says both 'welcome' and 'hurry up' at the same time.

I turn to Giulio, but he's in blank-faced unhelpful mode ... the one he defaults to when he's waiting for me to mess up. This time, it's choosing the right meal. I hate that he knows Nina's tastes better than I do. But then I remember Ma telling me about Ferragosto – a public holiday on the fifteenth of August where everyone in Italy takes the day off. Nina always took her to the beach at Santa Marinella with lasagna or *pasta al forno* as picnic food. Nina's motto being 'if it's not hot, it's not lunch' – which, come to think of it, must be why Giulio brings her meals.

Those dishes aren't on today's menu, though, so I choose the next best thing.

'*Pasta e fagioli, per favore.*' I'm clammy at the mere thought of this hot, soupy pasta. And even more so because Giulio hasn't reacted at all; his face gives nothing away.

I'm still second-guessing myself as we join the steady stream of visitors ferrying foil containers to the hospital, like a trail of ants bringing food to a nest – one that's filled with high-maintenance food snobs. The heat radiating from the takeaway bag is unbearable, and I must look ridiculous, marching down the corridor with my arms out, trying to keep the scalding warmth away from me.

Giulio raises an eyebrow. 'Interesting choice, Scotland.'

My smile verges on smug when, hands full, I turn to nudge Nina's door open with my hip and find myself face to face with him. 'Oh, I'm sorry, have I spoilt your fun?'

He looks confused.

'It's spoons all round today, Giulio. You won't get to make your favourite little joke.'

Giulio's laugh follows me into the room; a warm, genuine chuckle that leaves me momentarily stunned, aware just how much I like the sound of it. But more than that, I realize, I'm weirdly pleased to have been the one to coax it out of him.

Nina looks up from her bed, catching the exchange between us. Her smile is warmer than I've ever seen it, like she's approving of something more than just our food delivery. Maybe Isla's right. Maybe the way to Nina's heart really is through Giulio.

Before I can take another step, I notice someone at Nina's bedside – a familiar face I wasn't expecting to see here. Signora Pedretti is sitting on a plastic chair, a bag of oranges clasped in her lap.

'We brought lunch,' I say, setting it on the small table over Nina's bed. 'But if we're interrupting . . .'

'No interruption,' Nina says quickly, her smile vanishing. 'We've finished here.'

With a weary sigh, Signora Pedretti gets to her feet, only slightly taller now that she's standing. 'Just think about what I said, Adelina, *d'accordo*?'

Nina pouts. 'You mean, what *she* said.'

Signora Pedretti's lips barely move as she mutters, '*Dio*, give me strength,' before leaving the room with a brief nod in Giulio's and my direction.

Nina lifts one of the foil container lids and peers inside, inhaling deeply. '*Ah! Bene!* Proper food at last.' She smiles again, not quite the Botox-busting crinkly ones she reserves for Giulio, but she's slowly defrosting towards me – maybe it's my regular visits, or maybe because I'm saying more each time.

'So . . .' I clear my throat. 'What was Signora Pedretti talking about just now? Does she visit often?'

Nina's expression tightens, and I immediately regret asking.

'Not as often as she visits Caterina, it seems.' She practically snatches the bowl Giulio's offering her, and I notice the absence of the usual twinkle she gives him.

And Giulio . . . he's shifting about on his mattress perch like a scolded schoolboy.

'She loves our coffee,' he offers weakly.

'She loves to meddle, you mean. And now Caterina's got her doing her dirty work.'

Dirty work? The only dirty work Ma does involves kitty litter and a scoop. I search Nina's face for clues as she chases a cannellini bean around the tomatoey broth. I want to know what she means, and why Ma hasn't been back since her impromptu lunch trip on Giulio's Vespa – not even on Sunday – but my relationship with Nina still feels fragile, and I'm afraid it will shatter if I press too hard. I've only just started getting smiles. So I swallow my questions and focus on my food. Only, a few spoonfuls in, the heat of the dish starts to hit me, and I think I might melt on to the floor. What was I thinking, ordering *pasta e fagioli* during a heatwave?

Nina notices. 'Have you been outside at all, Livia? You will never get used to the sun if you hide away from it.'

I'm reminded of our first conversation, and how

pale she thinks I am. I shift so the overbed table hides my arms from her judgemental stare. 'I've been . . . busy. Language classes . . . the bar . . .'

Nina waves her spoon at Giulio again. '*Caro*, perhaps you can show Livia around a little?' Then, after a pause, she adds, 'When the bar is closed . . . so Caterina is not working alone.'

Is it my imagination, or is Nina eyeballing Giulio like she's trying to zap a secret message straight into his brain? Or maybe there are so many secrets flying around that I'm seeing them even where they don't exist.

18

When we turn into Via dei Serpenti, I spot a man in a smart navy suit pacing in front of the bar. He looks familiar, but before I can fully place him, Giulio veers sharply left, taking us up a side street. I grab his shoulders to keep my balance and find myself flattened against him, so close I feel the low vibration of his voice when he speaks.

'Just need to make a quick detour!'

'Giulio!' I protest, but he accelerates harder, only stopping when we're on a long avenue lined with ancient stone walls and broccoli-shaped trees, the rocks and ruins of the Roman Forum stretching out below us. Tourists crowd in around tour guides holding up colourful umbrellas to make themselves stand out in the throng. I'm surprised to see locals here, too – businesspeople on benches, talking loudly into their hands-free earpieces, families watching kids climbing on low walls.

I turn to Giulio. 'Why—'

'Nina wants you to see some of the sights,

remember?' he interrupts, tilting his chin towards the ruins, his voice casual, like he didn't just swerve away from the bar and the man standing outside it.

I cross my arms, frustration boiling over. 'You might think I'm some bumbling tourist, Giulio, but I'm not an idiot – that man back there . . . he was hanging around your Vespa the other day. Why are you avoiding him? And don't tell me this is a sightseeing detour.'

Giulio runs a hand through his hair, the bright sun picking out the golden tones, especially in the tufts that are left sticking up. I run a hand through my own to satisfy the strange urge to reach out and smooth his. I've just taken my helmet off, but the frizzy mass is already hot to touch. Maybe I'm overheating and that's why my brain's malfunctioning. It's like Nina says – I'm not used to the sun.

Giulio hoists himself on to a wall and kicks his heels against the stone. He's obviously trying to think of a good excuse. I can tell the moment he gives up, because he lets out a long sigh and his feet go still.

'That man . . . his name's Bertolli. He works for the bank, but he's got a thing for vintage Vespas and hinted he might accept the bike as a sort of down payment.'

'Down payment?' My confusion deepens. 'For what?'

'For the debts. To stop the bar being . . .' Giulio pauses, his voice dropping to a whisper. '*Pignorato.*'

'*Pignorato?* What does that mean?' For once, I don't care that I'm showing my lack of Italian vocabulary.

'The bank will take the bar away if the debt is not repaid in full,' he explains, his expression grim.

Repossessed. It means repossessed. But the word still doesn't make any sense. 'How can the bank do that? Nina owns the bar outright, and the flat above. Ma told me.'

Giulio shakes his head. 'Nina's been borrowing against the property to keep the business afloat. But she's fallen behind on the repayments. Far behind. I didn't know anything about it until she went into hospital and I had to deal with the post.'

I press a hand to my chest to ease the painful squeeze of my heart. The bar that's been in my family for generations is in danger of being taken away.

'You can't tell Nina the debt is being recalled . . . Not while she's in hospital.' Giulio's voice is urgent, his eyes seeking mine . . . holding my gaze. 'She needs to concentrate on getting better. I won't have her worrying that there might not be anything to come back to.'

My mind races. All those times I thought Giulio was up to something shady – the letter, stealing money from the till, snooping in the paperwork – I had it completely wrong. He wasn't taking from the bar; he was trying to save it. And I misjudged him. Completely.

Then there's that call I overheard on the rooftop – he must have been talking to Bertolli, telling him not to send the letters to the bar in case Ma found out.

'I get why you don't want to worry Nina, but why hide it from us?'

Giulio's lips twitch. 'You and I haven't exactly been friends.'

I squirm at his understatement. 'True . . . but . . . what's that got to do with Ma? If anything, she's always on your side.' I try to keep the bitterness from my voice.

'The thing is . . .' There's a pause, and now it's Giulio who's uncomfortable. 'Nina asked me to keep an eye on her, so I wasn't—'

'Wait.' I cut him off, my voice rising. 'You've been spying on Ma? For Nina? Are you kidding me?'

Giulio holds up his hands. 'No! It's not like that. Nina just asked me to report back on any . . . private meetings. That's all. And if it makes you feel any better, I haven't said anything.'

I narrow my eyes. 'Not even about Ma and Signora Pedretti's little chats?' Although, as I say it, I remember

Nina seeming to reprimand him about that very thing.

Giulio shakes his head. 'If Caterina knew about the debt, she'd go straight to Nina. And I want to come up with a solution first . . . if I can. I want to offer Nina hope, not add to her worries.'

I press my fingers to my temples, torn between the guilt of keeping Ma in the dark and the fear of burdening Nina when she's already vulnerable. 'So, what . . . we say nothing?'

'Buy some time with the Vespa, I suppose.' Giulio looks at the sky, his expression pained. 'Give Bertolli what he wants.'

'But it belonged to your nonna! Your *actual* family.' I surprise myself with the strength of my outburst. I mean, what do I care about his Vespa? Or him, for that matter.

Still, I don't like how Giulio's whole body shrinks away from me . . . or the challenge in his voice when he speaks. 'Nina and I might not be related by blood, but I told you, she's been there for me my whole life. I owe her.'

Sunshine gleams off the Vespa. 'So, you'd actually give it up?'

Giulio folds forwards, elbows on his knees. He mumbles, but I can't tell if it's because his chin is cupped in his hands or if he's reluctant to say the words. 'If it saves the bar . . . if it buys Nina more time . . . *allora sì*, I'll give it up.'

I believe him. He'd be willing to sacrifice something of his nonna's to help Nina . . . for *my* nonna. And while my feelings are tangled up about that, surprise knotted with jealousy, I'm all too aware I'm only here for the summer and not sure I have any right to be part of this at all.

'What if Ma already knows about the debts?' I blurt, grasping at straws.

'There's nothing in the paperwork she's been looking at, and I haven't heard her mention anything to your dad . . .' An uncharacteristic flush appears on Giulio's neck. 'I was trying to get information,' he adds, hurriedly. 'A way to help Nina – money I didn't know about. Anything.'

I fold my arms across my chest. He's been spying and eavesdropping, as I suspected all along. 'Are you keeping any more secrets? Do you know what Ma and Signora Pedretti have been whispering about?'

'I don't, Scotland. I promise. But Nina's right. Signora Pedretti loves to meddle. When you were in class, she had that new phone of hers out, asking me to video-call Flaminia. Then she remembered an "errand" and left us to it. Honestly, you'd think she bought that phone just to get us together.'

I swallow this information, but for some reason it sticks in my throat.

Unaware of my inner turmoil, Giulio slides off the wall.

'Come on, Scotland. I can't avoid Bertolli for ever. And now that you know, maybe you can help me.'

19

Bertolli's gone when we get back, and Giulio must be so relieved he doesn't even realize his body has sagged against mine, his back pressing softly against my front. But as soon as he parks in his usual spot, he tenses again – grip tightening on the handlebars, knuckles whitening.

'Wait here.' He steps off the Vespa and heads towards his apartment building, stopping at the mailboxes fixed to the outside wall.

Ignoring him, I follow close behind, my heart thudding in my chest as he pulls something from one of the slits. It's a torn scrap of paper with words scribbled across it, written in a hurry and shoved in without much care.

'Is it from Bertolli? What does it say?' I stand on my tiptoes and try to read the messy scrawl.

Giulio crumples the note in his fist. 'The offer to take the Vespa as payment is valid for two more weeks. After that, the bank will take legal action if we can't repay the debt in full.' He stares past me, his jaw tight.

I can tell he's looking at his Vespa, wondering how much longer it will belong to him.

I open my mouth to ask the question I've been putting off – to know exactly how much Nina owes – but Ma steps out of the bar.

That radar of hers? It's been programmed to alert her when I'm *this* close to *this* boy.

There's a faint pillow crease on her cheek; she must've been having a nap. She checks the smartwatch Pa bought her for Christmas – the one she still only uses to tell the time. 'I'm just reopening. You've been gone a while. Everything OK with Nina?'

Giulio's silent plea pokes into my back like a finger. *Don't tell her about the debts. Not yet.*

I usher Ma back inside, blinking at the shift from bright sunlight to the bar's dim interior. 'Actually, I think she smiled at me today.'

'Because I wasn't there to ruin her day,' Ma huffs, then waves her hand, trying to dismiss the comment.

'She was probably just happy about the *pasta e fagioli*, actually. But it's great she has an appetite, right?'

Ma nods, her smile a little tight. 'Appetite's one thing, but it takes more than a good meal to get back on your feet. Especially at her age.'

I hear Giulio's voice in my head – all the more reason not to dampen her spirits with hopeless news.

'Have you spoken to the doctors? Do you know when she's getting out?' And if she'll have a bar to come back to, I wonder – but keep that uncomfortable thought to myself.

'Getting up to the flat will be the biggest hurdle. But, knowing your nonna, she'd manage the stairs in a full body cast out of stubbornness alone.' She laughs at her own joke, but there's a bitter edge too.

I push a tiny bit more, but it's like I'm rolling out pasta dough – stretching it just thin enough to work, but not so much that it tears apart. 'What happened to make things so ... tense ... between you?'

Ma lets out a long breath. 'Let's just say she doesn't appreciate my interference.'

'But Giulio would be doing this all on his own if we hadn't come.'

Nooo. Cavolo! I've said the wrong thing. Ma's pupils dilate like a cat zeroing in on its target. And yep, that's me.

'*Aha!* You are warming to Giulio now, *si*?'

I want to scream into a pillow. I was getting so close to finding out the truth. My breath hisses out of me like steam from a boiling moka pot. 'I just mean ... we'll be back in Scotland soon enough, and Giulio goes back to school in September. Time's running out.'

In ways you don't even know. The secret burrows into the pit of my stomach. I could tell her right now – about the debt, about Bertolli, about the trouble the bar's in. It seems wrong not to. So wrong I open my mouth to let the words spill out . . . but then Ma's phone buzzes on the counter and Isla's name pops up on the screen.

Ma picks it up, cradling it in both hands as if she's worried she's going to press the wrong button by accident. Her expression goes all mushy when she sees the message.

'Aww, look at the little *micetti*.' She shows me pics of the two foster kittens that have just arrived at the cattery from the shelter she partners with. The tension of our conversation melts away as we coo over them, guessing which one's going to cause Isla the most trouble.

I point to the little tabby pictured with its claws in Isla's jumper. 'That one has a side parting like Enrico's. It'll probably want its own corner table and a cappuccino every morning.'

Ma laughs, and it's so nice to see the strain of the last two weeks leave her face that I don't want to ruin it by telling her about the debts. I have to get ready for language class, anyway. And, if I'm honest, it's also because of Giulio. He's willing to give up his Vespa for the bar, for Nina. The least I can do is keep quiet ... for a day or two at least. I'll tell her soon, I promise myself. There's still time to come up with a solution.

20

Giulio and I spend the next day doing everything we can think of – listing belongings online, applying for loans (a complete waste of time when you're under eighteen), and even a quick recce mission to the Trevi Fountain to see if dredging coins is a possibility (plenty of money, even more CCTV).

With no better ideas, we decide to double down on our spying efforts to uncover whatever Ma and Signora Pedretti are discussing.

Which is why my heart jumps when my friends and I arrive at the bar for our first language swap, and I find Ma and Signora Pedretti locked in an animated conversation – with Giulio loitering nearby.

We hold a quick exchange in eyebrow Morse code.

Eyebrow flick – *Hear anything useful?*

Slow lift of both brows – *Nothing yet.*

Quick double lift – *Keep trying!*

Single raised brow from Giulio – *I am!*

'Hey!' Ren tugs me down into the empty chair

beside him and reaches for the Tupperware container he's been lugging around all afternoon. He does a little drum roll on the lid before opening it up with a flourish. '*Voilà!*'

We peer inside, then at each other, unsure of what we're looking at.

Ren clucks his tongue. 'It's sushi caprese! Can't you tell?'

I look more closely. It *does* look like sushi. But instead of rice, there's a thin round of mozzarella at the bottom, a cherry tomato on top, and a thinly sliced strip of cucumber where the seaweed would be. I think there's even a drizzle of balsamic glaze acting like it's soy sauce.

I react the way I should have the moment Ren did his big reveal. 'Wow! They look amazing.'

Sofia opens the camera on her phone and takes a close-up before popping one in her mouth. Then she pushes her chair back and stands. 'I will get Giulio to model one – to make the picture even tastier!' Suddenly, I struggle to swallow my own mouthful.

She carries the container to the counter, holding it high like a waiter in a fancy restaurant. 'Chef Ren invites you to try his *famoso* sushi caprese. *É bom!*'

Giulio holds one up to the light. 'I don't know who's going to be more offended – the Japanese or the Italians.'

Ren grins. 'You sound like my parents.' He adopts a high-pitched French accent and pretends to flip his hair. 'Why change something that is already perfect?' Then he folds his arms across his chest and dips his chin, his voice deepening. 'This is not the Japanese way.'

Kenzi, Sofia and I share a moment of understanding at Ren's imitation of his parents – we know exactly what it's like to be caught in a cultural crossfire.

It's almost strange speaking English again, after only using it with Isla, but Kenzi and I chat easily now that we're free from the stilted role-playing of class. She tells me about her brother Mehdi's citizenship application, how he's struggling to find a long-term job to boost his chances. And when it's my turn to speak Italian, I keep it light – about life in Edinburgh, mostly. How bidets are NOT the norm, and umbrellas are pointless because the wind makes the rain horizontal. I'd love to fill Kenzi in on what I know about the bar, but not when Ma's within earshot.

Sofia drifts in and out, occasionally giving Signora Pedretti tips on how to use her new mobile – even though Signora Pedretti's elected Giulio as her tech guru. I don't even notice the time passing until Ma starts dropping some not-too-subtle hints that it's time to close – it starts with her noisily cleaning the coffee machine and ends with her shooing everyone out so she can lock up and mop the floor without our footprints ruining it all.

I float up to the apartment, giddy from the success of the swap. The bar felt less like a backdrop and more like a part of my life – even if I was on the wrong side of the counter.

Kenzi and I were the ones doing it properly, actually making an effort with the whole language thing. Ren was fine until Enrico showed up to test his snacks, but redeemed himself when Signora Pedretti accidentally switched her phone settings to Japanese. And Sofia? Well, she has too much faith in Signora Pedretti being able to follow her 'handy shortcuts'.

I'm grinning when I slump on to the sofa. It looks old, but the cushions are firm and the textured fabric doesn't have any worn patches. I get the impression this room rarely gets used and that, like our house in Edinburgh, the kitchen is the real hub. There's a long, low coffee table between the sofa and a dusty TV screen, the corner of an envelope poking out of a single drawer just under the tabletop. My mind races – could it be something from the bank? A final notice, maybe? Or something worse? I wince as the drawer creaks open, expecting to see formal paperwork or an official letterhead. Instead, the envelope is part of a bundle, neatly tied together with a length of string. They're not bills or statements, though. They're personal . . . I recognize the handwriting instantly. Those neat, rounded letters, the fancy Gs and slanted As I've seen on shopping lists and notes attached to the fridge door at home.

My breath catches. These are letters from Ma to Nina.

21

Before I can stop myself, I shove the bundle of letters under my T-shirt and slip into the privacy of my Giulio-themed bedroom. I sit on the edge of the bed and quickly untie the string holding them together.

The first one is dated nearly ten years ago, which must have been shortly after our last family visit to Rome. It's short, just a page, but it starts with an apology.

Mamma, I'm sorry for what happened. I don't know how to fix this, but I'm trying. Please answer my calls.

An apology? From Ma? She never apologizes. Not in words, anyway. Her medium is food; *tagliatelle al ragù* if the apology is for me, and some awful Roman offal dish for Pa — an apology that stinks out the kitchen for days and has the cats scratching at the connecting door to get in. Thankfully, Ma doesn't apologize to Pa all that often.

So it's surreal, reading through the rest of the letters, finding apology after apology and Ma begging

Nina to get in touch. There's other stuff, too – little glimpses into our lives in Edinburgh like when Ma started up Caterina's Cat Casa and was worried about making a go of it, about how difficult it is when Pa's away on shoots . . . and loads about me growing up and starting school. But the same thread of apologies runs through every letter – *Scusami, Mamma. Perdonami*.

I make sure to keep the envelopes in the same order they were tied in, all ten years' worth. And yet, in all that time, I don't remember any letters arriving from Nina, apart from birthday cards for me. My chest tightens at the thought of Ma reaching out, trying to fix something I didn't even know about. Something I *still* don't know about.

I lean back against the wall, accidentally dislodging a photo from the collage. It flutters on to the bed and I pick it up to find it's one of a younger Giulio, standing next to the blue Vespa with a woman who must be his nonna. The Vespa looks like it does now – Giulio clearly takes care of it. Guilt gnaws at me. He's been upfront with me about the debts, about being prepared to sell his nonna's Vespa to help save the bar. I need to share this with him too. I know the letters aren't about the debts, but they are about Ma and Nina – and it's their constant bickering and sniping that's holding me back from opening up to Ma. How can I tell her Nina's in debt without making things a hundred times worse between them? And, much as I hate to admit it, Giulio knows Nina better than I do, so maybe he knows how to help with this too.

It's nearly midnight when Ma finally heads to bed. But I wait another half hour before sneaking up to the rooftop. The night air is warm, the cityscape bathed in golden lamplight, still alive with people enjoying the summer evening. I climb over the low railing on to Giulio's side of the terrace and, after a little pep talk from Inner Isla, I knock on his door ... so gently I have to do it a second time. Louder ... in tune with my hammering heart.

There's a pause, then the sound of footsteps. Then Giulio's tall shape appears in the doorway, silhouetted against the light from inside. His face is hard to read in the shadows, but I can tell he's surprised.

'Couldn't wait until morning to see me, Scotland?' he murmurs, his voice low as he joins me outside.

'I need your help.' I hold up the bundle of envelopes. 'I found these letters from Ma to Nina, full of apologies.'

Music drifts up from somewhere nearby – probably from the piazza with the octagonal fountain at the bottom of the road. I think back to wandering past it with my case that first night, looking and feeling like an outsider, then drag my attention back to Giulio.

He frowns at the letters in my hand. 'What's she apologizing for?'

'That's the thing, see? She doesn't say... it's like she doesn't have to, as if Nina will definitely know.' I shake my head in frustration. 'Ma started sending them after our last trip to Rome ten years ago. Something must have happened then. I... I was wondering if you knew anything?'

I unfold one, scanning it quickly to make sure there's nothing embarrassing about me in it. Once I'm sure it's safe, I hand it to Giulio. His long, straight eyelashes almost brush his cheeks as he skims the letter. I clear my throat, grateful it's too dark for him to see the tide of warmth flooding my cheeks.

I find a point on the horizon and stare at it, breathing in for the count of four and out for the count of six... remembering the technique from some well-being class at school, hoping it will return my face to its normal colour.

'This doesn't really tell us anything.' He holds out the letter and I make an effort not to brush against his fingers when I take it from him.

It hits me suddenly – what if Giulio thinks I've dragged him out here for nothing? That this is just an excuse to... see him?

I try to make him understand. 'It's vague, I know. But something happened. Ma never apologizes ...'

'Isn't that just adults, though?' Giulio scoffs. 'My parents never say sorry. It's the one thing they have in common.'

I go still, as if I've stumbled across a wild creature and don't want to scare it away. It's the first time Giulio's brought up his parents without Ma asking about them.

'Sometimes I wonder if it's because Papà is from the north, and Mamma's from the south,' Giulio says, his voice thoughtful.

I raise an eyebrow. 'I thought your mum was from Rome?'

He rolls his eyes. 'Anything below Florence is the south for Papà.'

I can't help but laugh a little at that, some of the tension dissolving. A north–south divide ... I hadn't considered it before. But before I can think any more about it, Giulio points at the letters in my hands and says, '*Allora* ... what do we do now?'

'I need to tell Ma about the debts ...'

He frowns, opening his mouth like he's about to protest.

'But I want to speak to Signora Pedretti first,' I finish. 'You've seen what Ma and Nina are like. There's so much tension. Ma's not even going to lunch any more, and now these letters. There's something bigger here. So I was thinking . . .' I hurry on. 'Maybe you could distract Ma the next time Signora Pedretti's in, and I could talk to her . . . see if she'll open up? She obviously knows something, and spying's getting us nowhere.'

Giulio nods. I start to move away, then the opening notes to a classic Italian power ballad drift up over the rooftops, one I recognize from Pa's favourite Spotify list.

'Vasco Rossi,' I say with a small smile.

Giulio looks at me in surprise. 'This song is famous in Scotland?'

I laugh. 'Err, no. Definitely not. But my dad loves this track. He plays it a lot.'

I peer over the balustrade, aware of Giulio's gaze lingering on my profile for a long moment before he looks too. We can't actually see the fountain or who is playing the music, but we stand there until the song is finished, half-singing, heads nodding, in the moment. Together.

22

After three hours of Italian weather vocabulary, when the only word we're likely to use is *rovente* – scorching! – I'm more convinced than ever that Kenzi's language swap is the way to go if I'm ever going to pass for one of the locals.

And it's an added bonus that Signora Pedretti is already perched on her usual stool when we arrive at the bar. Predictably, however, Ma's right in front of her, getting in the way as usual.

I sense Giulio trying to catch my eye and we fall into our usual silent communication.

He wiggles an eyebrow and tilts his head in Ma's direction – *need a distraction?*

I nod, then second-guess our telepathic powers when, instead of heading for Ma, he disappears outside. But then, moments later, he reappears in the doorway. 'Caterina . . . the sun umbrella's broken . . . looks like the pin's come out. Can you give me a hand?'

Ma frowns. '*Com'è possibile?* How did that happen?'

Giulio shrugs, but when Ma walks past him, he looks towards me for a split second, eyebrows rising a tiny fraction. I suppress a smile; he must have sabotaged it on purpose.

While everyone else is distracted by Ren's new fusion delicacy – a French *croque monsieur* made with Italian ciabatta bread that has Sofia whipping her phone out to snap photos – I slip behind the counter and stand opposite Signora Pedretti, my mind racing for a way to interrogate her over Ma and Nina's relationship as I uncap some fizzy soft drinks for us.

'So . . . do you visit Nina often? I've never seen you at the hospital before.' I dive straight in.

Signora Pedretti looks guarded but answers. 'Not often, no.'

I sigh. 'More than Ma, I bet. I really wish they hadn't fallen out so badly.'

Signora Pedretti takes a slow sip of her drink. 'You know about that?'

'How could I not? It's like they're opponents in a boxing ring, only they're throwing insults instead of punches. I mean, we've stayed away for ten years. I can't imagine that happening to me and Ma, but . . .'

I can't finish the sentence. I might have engineered this conversation, but that doesn't make the loss any less real . . . the ache any less painful.

Signora Pedretti's face softens. 'There was a misunderstanding, *cara*. Although your nonna considers it more . . . a betrayal.'

'A betrayal?' I echo, not liking the sound of the word at all. 'Why? Because Ma moved to Scotland?'

She tilts her head as if she's considering it. 'Partly, yes, I believe so. Adelina is deeply rooted in this city. She was still a young woman when your nonno died, and Caterina is her only daughter. But there is more to it than that . . .'

My breath catches; this is it . . . I'm finally going to learn the truth . . .

Then Ma bursts in, the top part of her hair bouncing weirdly as she walks. 'I fixed the umbrella with my clip!' She beams at us with pride. 'Like MacGyver.'

Mistaking my sigh of frustration for confusion – which, weirdly, is also accurate – her hands go to her hips.

'Or that girl . . . the one on YouTube who fixes everything with stuff from her handbag.'

I raise an eyebrow. 'Lucy the Lifehacker?'

'*Esatto!*' Ma grins.

Giulio joins me behind the counter and holds up a small metal pin so that only I can see. 'What do I do with this?'

'Give it to Ma,' I scowl. 'She can fix the Leaning

Tower of Pisa or something.'

Opportunity to dig over, I add a twist of lemon to our drinks and round the counter to carry them over.

Ren leaps up. 'Allow me, *mademoiselle*.'

But as he goes to take the tray, Giulio snatches it away. 'That's my job.' His jaw is tense as he sets the glasses on the table among the food clutter, but before I can inspect the reason for it, Sofia's excited voice breaks into my thoughts.

'Hey! Someone's sent a message on Ren's page.'

Ren cranes his neck. 'I have a page?'

'You do now.' Sofia shows us a beautiful photo grid of Ren's culinary creations. 'I set it up the other day.'

'What is it? Do they want me on *MasterChef* or something?'

Giulio snickers quietly and I glare at him.

'Umm, it's in Italian so I don't really understand it, but I don't think it's that,' Sofia answers carefully. 'The guy who messaged has a pretty big following, though – almost as many as I do.'

Kenzi takes the phone, skim-reading the text as she translates, simplifying the message. 'It's about a food tour of Rome ... hang on, there's a link.'

Ren hangs an arm over my shoulder as we all lean in.

'It's on Sunday,' Kenzi continues. 'Basically, they're

offering the chance to go on a sightseeing tour for foodies!'

'Nice!' Sofia says. 'See what a little bit of social media posting can get you!'

Ren spins me to face him. 'You should come, Livia. You haven't done any sightseeing, yet.'

I flinch, wishing Ren hadn't said that in front of everyone . . . like I'm a tourist-in-waiting.

Before I can think of a polite excuse, Giulio clears his throat. 'Sundays are busy here. We need Livia to help.'

I'm surprised but pleased he thinks I'm actually useful. Ma, however, who has the hearing of a cat, pounces on the opportunity to send me sightseeing.

'Giulio, *caro*. Why don't you show Livia around? If Nina wasn't in hospital, she would do it herself . . . I bet she took you to all her favourite spots.'

I can think of a spot or two I'd show Giulio, Inner Isla murmurs.

But her joke doesn't quell the little bubble of jealousy swelling inside me. It's not Giulio's fault I wasn't here, I remind myself. But still, if I had Nina in my life when I was growing up, I wouldn't be here now, feeling like a loose part half the time.

Giulio shifts his weight from one foot to the other. 'I suppose I could. Maybe Saturday afternoon . . . if you don't mind managing alone for a while.'

I brace for one of Ma's cringey comments, but she surprises me by being normal and simply nodding.

Kenzi leans over, her voice low. 'You and Giulio? Sightseeing together? What have I missed?'

A lot, I realize. The reason she and the others came to the bar in the first place was to help me spy on Giulio – she has no idea we're working together now, trying to find a solution to the debts, Giulio's plan to sell his Vespa, and whether or not to tell Ma everything.

'It's a long story,' I say, half-laughing, half-sighing. 'I'll fill you in on Monday at class.'

So much has shifted in such a small amount of time. Even the bar feels livelier than it did two weeks ago. A couple of twenty-somethings hover at the entrance, their eyes straying to the now half-eaten goodies on our table – proof that we're making something happen here . . . something I didn't think was possible.

23

When Giulio and I leave the hospital the next day, I'm not thinking about our impossible deadline for once. With my belly full of *gnocchi alla Sorrentina*, and my heart full of the progress I'm making with Nina, the stress of having to come up with a whole lot of cash in only nine days is briefly overshadowed by my recent wins. Small ones, but I'll take them.

Nina didn't flinch once at my accent. She even complimented me on the green cami I bought from a local market, telling me she likes to shop there too. And the only time the tiniest crease appeared in the artificially smooth skin of her forehead was when I told her Giulio was going to show me some of her favourite places in the city, and she asked if Ma would be alone at the bar. She must still be worried about Ma having secret meetings. Or maybe it's to do with the betrayal Signora Pedretti mentioned. I still haven't told Giulio about that. Right before seeing Nina was hardly the best time, and bringing it up as I climb on to the Vespa isn't either.

My feet automatically find the fold-out pegs to rest on. The dip of the suspension adjusting to my weight is familiar now too, but I'll never get used to the feeling of my knees brushing against his legs, or how the warmth of his body through his T-shirt makes me all floaty inside. It's the heatwave, of course, and the helmet trapping the sweltering air around me, making me light-headed.

At first, I think we're going to the Bocca della Verità, the giant stone face that's rumoured to bite off the hands of liars who dare to put their fingers in its open mouth. But he drives straight past the long queue of people waiting to see if the legend is true. I'm relieved — not because I've been lying to Ma about the bar's debts but because I'm just not comfortable being around the big tourist traps. I don't want to feel like an outsider.

Instead, we park a short distance away on the Aventine, and I hear Ma's preachy voice in my head. *This is one of the Seven Hills on which Rome was built, Livia!*

Between Ma and Inner Isla, I think I might need to see a doctor.

Giulio leads me to Il Giardino degli Aranci, a public park with rows of orange trees, their sweet, citrusy scent almost too much in the warm air. He walks just ahead, clearly trying to build suspense. I'm about to call him out on it, but then we reach the end of the path and, when he finally moves aside, I stop dead. Rome is *right* there, laid out in all its glory – hills, monuments, ruins and modern buildings – all wobbling in a heat haze.

'It's SO beautiful.' I lean out over the wall, drinking it all in.

'It is,' Giulio says quietly. But his eyes are on me.

My stomach does that weird little flip. I turn back to the view, but my every nerve-ending stays with him, hyper-tuned to his slightest movement.

He clears his throat. 'Historical lasagna.'

'Huh?' The blood whooshing in my veins must be messing with my hearing.

'It's how Nina describes Rome. Layers and layers of history, built one on top of the other . . . like a lasagna.'

'Well, that fits . . . what with Rome and food being her two favourite things.' I freeze, my own words taking me by surprise. I know this about Nina. Not because of something Ma or Giulio has said but from my own experience of her, from our daily lunch visits.

I trace the path of the river Tiber to the small island where the hospital sits, its peachy-orange walls just visible through the trees. My connection to Nina stretches over the city . . . a bit stronger than it was before.

'Historical lasagna . . .' I try out the words. Nina's words. 'Sounds like something Ren would cook up.'

'So, will he be coming to the bar every night?'

I frown at the shift in Giulio's tone. 'Is that a problem? Some new people looked like they were about to come in yesterday. I think it helps having Ren and my friends there.'

Giulio follows a crack in the paving with the toe of his trainer. 'What's the point in new customers if he's giving food away for free? Not exactly helping Nina's profits, is it?'

'If more people come, they might buy . . .' I start to defend my friend, but I see Giulio looking back the way we came, to where his Vespa is parked, a muscle pulsing in his clenched jaw.

'Oh! I still haven't filled you in on yesterday. When you distracted Ma with the sun umbrella, I spoke to Signora Pedretti. She said something about a "misunderstanding" between Ma and Nina . . . something about Nina feeling betrayed.'

Giulio gasps. 'Betrayed? By Caterina?'

'Well, we know Ma's been apologizing for something . . .' I bundle my hair into a ponytail and fan the back of my neck. 'But then Ma did that whole hair-clip hack before I could get the whole story.' I sigh, frustrated. 'And I can't tell if it's serious enough that we shouldn't trust her with the truth about the debts. I mean . . . we're talking about my mum – she's all about cats and romcom marathons and . . . unsolicited advice about kissing boys.'

I did *not* mean to say that last one.

Giulio smirks and lifts a brow.

I keep mine super still – *I'm not going there.*

He raises the other, daring me to keep going.

I fold my arms, adding a slight frown to double down on my point. *Nope. Not happening.*

A smile tugs at his lips and he pushes away from the wall. 'Come on, Scotland. There's one more thing I want to show you.'

We leave the orange garden and walk for a while, arms swinging at our sides, *almost* touching, until Giulio stops beside a huge green door set into a high wall.

He points to the small brass keyhole. 'Have a look through there.'

'What, so someone can poke me in the eye . . . or squirt water at me?'

He laughs, that rich, belly-warming sound again. 'Trust me, Scotland.'

With a jolt, I realize I do trust him. And that, even

if it is a prank, it won't be a cruel one.

I barely have to crouch to press my eye against the keyhole. At first, all I see is a blurry darkness. Then, as my sight adjusts, an image comes into focus. It's so vivid, I think someone's slotted a postcard into the keyhole, like a photo in a locket. But birds are swooping in the clear blue sky, which means the dome of St Peter's Basilica, perfectly framed by a path of arching greenery, is actually real. For a moment, the world narrows to just this – no bar, no debts, no secrets. Just this tiny, hidden view of one of Rome's most famous landmarks.

'This is . . . amazing,' I say, glancing back at Giulio.

He shrugs. 'Nina would've shown you if she wasn't in hospital. I'm just standing in for her.'

Of course. I blush, reminding myself that this is about Nina, not us. I mean . . . there *is* no us.

24

Our next stop is the Basilica di San Clemente, or to quote Giulio – 'a slice of the best historical lasagna in Rome'.

He's not joking.

We descend from a twelfth-century church to a fourth-century basilica below, then down again into an ancient Roman house and temple. *Actual* layers of history sitting one on top of the other.

Back on the Vespa, we whizz past crowded buses and trams and, though it feels like someone's blowing a hairdryer in my face, it's hands-down the best way to get around the city and is worth more than its vintage charm and the price tag Bertolli has put on it. It is pure freedom.

But there's no getting away from the blistering sun and the press of people when we park the Vespa and step into a piazza dominated by the massive dome of the Pantheon. A dozen different languages buzz in my ear, and I realize July has slipped into August – the absolute worst month to go near any of the big sights.

Sensing my panic at the wall of tourists ahead, Giulio reaches for my hand, pausing to check he isn't touching my fading burn. 'Stay close, OK?'

Swit swoo! Inner Isla catcalls in my ear as the low rumble of his voice makes me jump inside. The thrum of my heart pulses in my fingertips and I wonder if Giulio can feel it too. Relief floods through me as he steers us away from the crowds funnelling into the Pantheon, and down a narrow side street into an unexpected pocket of calm.

'It's not the Pantheon.' He pulls me inside a much smaller, tucked-away church. 'But it has a pretty impressive dome of its own.'

Intrigued, I tilt my head back, taking in the striking fresco curving high overhead, a masterpiece of angels and saints rising into a dramatic sky. My attention's only half on it though ... that hand, still lightly holding mine, is distracting. When he lets go to turn in a full circle, his eyes never leaving the ceiling, my relief is almost immediate, as if his touch had been sapping my focus. Although, honestly, there's a smidge of disappointment there too.

'See it yet?' he asks.

I squint up at the fresco, trying to figure out what 'it' is.

Giulio steps closer, and points to a spot above us.

'Look at the edges, see how the lines don't quite meet? That's how you can tell it's flat.'

I see it. The borders of the fresco blur, not quite connecting like they should. 'Oh,' I breathe, as the illusion falls away. He's right. The ceiling is flat, but the painting tricks the eye, making it seem like it's arching above us.

I sneak a look at Giulio and, not for the first time today, I feel like I'm seeing him in an unexpected way too. I give myself a mental kick. Giulio's just a stand-in.

'Thanks for showing me another of Nina's finds,' I say, more as a reminder to myself.

'Actually, this is one of my mum's favourite spots.' He pauses, kneading the heel of one hand into his shoulder as if he's loosening some tension. 'My dad never came, though.'

'Too busy driving lorries?'

'Yeah . . . it gets him away from Rome. He only moved here for my mum. Says everything's better in Milan – cleaner streets, trams are on time, blah, blah, blah.'

I snort. 'It's like my parents . . . they *choose* to live in Edinburgh but still complain non-stop about the weather . . . and the food. *Ommioddio.* Always the food.'

Giulio laughs. 'My dad says it's impossible to find a

decent *cotoletta alla Milanese* in this city.'

'Isn't that just veal in breadcrumbs?'

'*Sì*, but apparently it doesn't taste the same here . . .' He circles his hand around. 'The air . . . it's different.'

'Bet he moans about the coffee too, then.'

'The water changes the taste!' Giulio and I say at the same time, laughing in surprise at our shared thought, eyes meeting in mutual understanding.

The silence between us as we walk back to the Vespa is a comfortable one. We've only ever talked about the bar, or Nina. And maybe that's why today feels different. I've seen the real Rome from unexpected angles, and now I'm seeing him in a new way too – Giulio, who has his own family complications, his own stuff to deal with that doesn't involve Nina or the problems waiting for us at the bar.

By the time we head back, my footsteps land more heavily on the ground, like I belong here a little more. For the first time since arriving in Rome, I feel like less of a tourist – even though I've spent all afternoon visiting the sights.

25

Giulio parks up in his usual spot just as the streetlamps come on in Via dei Serpenti. One of the bar's arched wooden doors is pulled shut, a broom resting against it – a sure sign Ma's started closing up for the day.

Giulio checks the time on his phone. 'We've been out longer than I thought.'

I bite my lip, not because I think Ma will have struggled but because I remember the look on Nina's face when she heard Ma would be alone at the bar. Question is – was she worried about Ma not managing, or about Giulio not being there to keep an eye on her?

Ma's voice floats over to us as we approach the door. 'I can't do that to her . . . not again. But what other choice do I have? She won't listen to Signora Pedretti . . . and, as far as I can tell, the takings don't cover the overheads, let alone anything else.'

Giulio and I stop dead in our tracks, eyes locked. Ma doesn't know about the debts, but she's starting to put the pieces together — and if she keeps digging, it's only a matter of time before she hits, well, a big gaping hole where a lot of money has gone missing.

There's a pause, and then I hear Pa; his voice is tinny, like it's being filtered through a small speaker. 'If she can't keep things going—'

'But she has!' Ma interrupts. 'I just don't understand how.'

She props her phone against the coffee machine and moves to the side, using the steam from the milk frother to dampen the cloth in her hand. As she steps out of the frame, Pa spots me lurking in the doorway.

'Livia!' His face fills the screen as he leans in, as if that will bring us closer. I recognize our kitchen units behind him.

Ma spins round, a whole wheel of emotions turning over her face — surprise, pleasure, worry, guilt — before finally coming to rest on something resembling the expression of a cat toying with a mouse, right before it goes in for the kill.

Her voice is worryingly casual as she angles her phone to give Pa a better view. 'You remember Giulio, *vero*? Well, this pair have been gone so long I was beginning to think they'd eloped . . . like a modern-day Romeo and Juliet . . . or should that be Romea and Giulio?'

That's it. I'm dead.

The elopement joke is bad enough, but Ma's pun takes it to another level of parental embarrassment. She's positively glowing with pride, too.

Giulio makes a noise that's somewhere between a groan and a yelp, and I have to get him out of here right now – without looking at him, touching him, or even acknowledging his existence – because, clearly, Ma needs *no* encouragement.

Pa sighs. 'They remind me of us back in the day, *vero*, Caterina?'

And now I'm actually dead.

I lunge for the phone, finger poised over the red circle that will end the call and my humiliation.

Ma pulls away with a laugh. 'All right, all right. I'll stop.' She turns Pa back to face her. 'Call you later, *amore*!' She pouts at the screen and makes a string of loud kissy noises.

I drag a hand down my face. Ma goes on and on (and on!) about how natural it is to fall in love, but she's the one who's going to send any boy I'm remotely interested in running for the hills – all seven of them.

Giulio backs out into the street. 'I'll . . . umm . . . leave you to it.'

I lean over the counter to gather the empty glass

bottles to take out to the recycling bin, not expecting to find any but desperate for an excuse to be busy, and I find myself staring at a cluster of empty Crodino bottles — the aromatic, orange-coloured soft drink pensioners seem to enjoy before meals. 'Busy today?'

Ma pings open the drawer to the till, ready to start cashing up. 'The usual suspects. And Enrico brought someone new. A woman who wanted to thank your friend Kenzi. Something about helping with a prescription? I think he was hoping to snag some of Ren's snacks, too. If you let me finish here, we can take a walk together. Maybe visit the cat sanctuary where Julius Caesar was assassinated, get some pizza on the way?'

Only Ma can fit cats, food and Roman history into one sentence.

As we head out, the sun has fully set, but the air is only slightly cooler. Ma slows near the octagonal fountain. There's already music playing and she looks at the young people sitting on the ledge and the steps surrounding it with a fond smile. 'This is where your Pa and I had our first kiss.'

Ommioddio. I scramble for the Italian way to say TMI but, unsurprisingly, it's not a phrase Ma or Pa have ever taught me. I make a mental note to ask Giulio, almost losing my footing when I realize things really have changed between us if I'm prepared to go to him for language advice.

I wonder if Ma's noticed too, because she nudges an elbow into my ribs.

'It's a nice spot, no? You know, in case you're thinking of starting a new family tradition.'

26

The city is still in the grip of a heatwave when we open the bar on Sunday morning and though I'm dying to turn the air conditioning on, I know better now. The regulars would be back faster than you can say 'head cold', handing over their chiropractor bills and moaning about the Arctic conditions. But that's not the only progress I've been making. Not one customer has asked me where I come from and, even better, they drink their coffee without that nervous little pause first, like they're worried I'm going to poison their taste buds.

Giulio's just finished setting out olives and bite-size pieces of pizza and focaccia for the post-Mass rush but, as it's a lull right now, he's watching me froth the milk for his cappuccino – a cappuccino *he* asked *me* to make for him. Is it a trap? A test? Probably . . . which is why I am determined to make this the best cappuccino. Ever.

I tilt the cup as I pour in the milk, focusing on creating a simple leaf pattern. It's basic, but I've finally got the hang of it. I slide it along the counter, struggling to keep the smugness out of my smile. 'For you!'

Giulio reaches for the cup, then presses his hand to his chest instead. '*Per me?* Are you trying to tell me something, Scotland?'

Confused, I glance at the foam, my stomach dropping when I see my carefully crafted leaf has bloomed into a perfect heart shape – so perfect I couldn't have made it if I tried. '*No, cavolo!* That's not . . . I mean . . .' I jab the cup, hoping to muddy the design, but the heart only grows bigger. I groan. 'It's supposed to be a leaf.'

Giulio raises one dark brow, and I curse our eyebrow Morse code.

'You know that spoon you're always going on about? I think I need it after all.' I reach for the teaspoon on the saucer, but Giulio catches my hand just as I grab it, a grin spreading across his face.

'Oh no you don't, Scotland. Your heart is mine now.'

'Never!' I hold on tight, deliberately raising my voice a few notches. 'Giulio, let go! My burn—'

He lets go of me. Instantly. '*Oddio!* Did I hurt you?'

I plunge the teaspoon into the cup. 'Nah! Just kidding! That stopped hurting ages ago.' I stir until the foam dissolves into a beige swirl – but before I can gloat properly, Ma comes through the connecting door and I jump back as if I've been caught in a romantic clinch, even though Giulio is on the other side of the counter. *That's because you're worried she can read your thoughts, Liv.*

Inner Isla's timing is as inconvenient as Ma's.

I shake my head, as if ridding myself of a persistent little mosquito, and turn gratefully to the customers who are trickling in. But I stay buoyant for the rest of the morning.

It's my most successful day yet. Over half the tables are occupied and my croissant-recognition skills are improving with every order. But, best of all, I'm actually contributing, instead of causing problems with my 'foreign ways'.

It stays busy right up to lunchtime, until the mouth-watering smells of Sunday specials waft out of every open window in the street, luring customers away like children by the Pied Piper.

Giulio dumps a tray of dirty cups on the counter, the clash and clatter loud in the now-empty bar. 'You did well today, Scotland.'

A bubble of hope grows inside me. 'It was so busy! This could make a difference, right?' I lower my voice to a whisper. 'To Bertolli, I mean.'

Giulio shrugs. 'It was busy last Sunday too, remember? And the one before that. It's always our best day ... but it doesn't make up for the rest of the week. This afternoon it will all be back to normal.'

My little bubble bursts. He's right. But this was my first time seeing it from behind the counter, rather than behind a tray of dirty cups.

Ma unlatches one of the wooden doors and pulls it shut, casting shadows that mirror the sinking feeling in my chest. Silly, really, to think one busy morning could change anything.

She helps load the last of the cups into the washer, then dries her hands on a towel, her expression unreadable. I've been badgering her for days to have Sunday lunch with Nina again, like she'd planned to in the beginning, but now that she's agreed, I feel more like I've cornered her than convinced her.

'Can you go ahead and pick up lunch, Giulio? Livia and I will meet you at the hospital.' Her tone is flat, like she knows this won't be a cosy visit.

Ma and I take a bus this time, the streets strangely quiet with the restful Sunday feeling I don't see in Edinburgh. And even though we're above ground, she doesn't point out a single landmark or offer any 'fun facts' about Rome like she usually would. In fact, the closer we get to the hospital, the more she sinks into the hard plastic seat.

Giulio is already there, dishing out plates of *pasta al*

forno, fighting with the long strings of melting mozzarella that threaten to drag across the table. We exchange quick looks, and I know he's as on edge as I am.

'*Ciao*, Mamma.' Ma takes a plate of baked pasta and sits on one of the visitor's chairs. Same as last time, she faces Nina, but her body and feet point towards the door like she wants to bolt.

Nina's eyes analyse Ma, calculating. 'Caterina, how lovely of you to come in person ... instead of sending Signora Pedretti to do your bidding.'

Ma gulps down a mouthful of her lunch then bangs her fist against her chest as if it's stuck there. Her voice is croaky when she answers. 'I don't know what you mean, Mamma.'

Nina scoffs. 'Don't you? She seemed quite convinced I should consider ... retiring, and I thought to myself ... now where have I heard that before?'

'You're ten years older now, Mamma. Are you going to work for ever? The bar isn't just sitting behind a counter – it's a physical job.' She waves at Nina's leg, still suspended in the sling.

Nina's perfectly smooth forehead creases slightly, a movement so subtle I'd have missed it if I wasn't paying close attention – which I most definitely am.

'I'm not dead yet, Caterina. And there are plenty

of capable older people in this country . . . it's our Mediterranean diet.'

Ten years older now, that's what Ma said. Ten years older than when the apology letters began, ten years older than the last time we came to Rome. I look down at my plate, at my white-knuckled hand gripping my fork. Am I finally going to find out what happened all those years ago?

Giulio shifts on the bed. He's thinking the same thing I am.

Ma breaks the silence, her voice a little tight. 'Well, talking of diets, can we just try to enjoy our lunch?' She forces a smile at me and Giulio. 'You two were out all afternoon yesterday, weren't you? Why don't you tell Nina what you saw?'

A flicker of disapproval crosses Nina's face as she looks at Giulio; we left Ma to handle everything alone. But then, with a sigh, she relents, her gaze shifting to me. 'Where did you go?'

'The Giardino degli Aranci,' I say, leaping on the opportunity to lighten the atmosphere. 'The view was breathtaking. And the Basilica di San Clemente – Giulio was telling me about your historical lasagna theory.'

Her chin dips in a satisfied nod. 'Yes, you've caught a bit of colour. And your accent has improved.' She takes a sip of water, then turns back to Ma. 'It's a shame you didn't take her to these places, Caterina.'

Ma shifts to the very edge of her seat. 'I've been busy managing the bar.'

'Yes, well . . . I hope that's all you've been doing in my absence.'

There it is again, the insinuation Ma's been up to something behind her back.

And with that, Ma's up on her feet. 'We should get going.'

Nina smirks. 'Already?'

'Yes.' Ma's tone is firm. 'I have errands to run.'

Giulio stands too, clearly grateful for the out . . . but he offers me one as well. 'I can take Livia back on the Vespa.'

I nod, eager to escape the thick air in the room.

In the hallway, I pick up my pace to match Ma's. '*Ehi*, are you OK?'

She touches my arm. 'I'm fine, *tesoro*.'

I don't believe her for a second.

And she knows that, because she avoids meeting my eyes. 'I need to stop by the market before we reopen. I'll see you later, *va bene*?'

I nod again, but much as she tries to hide it . . . everything – Nina, the letters, the strained conversations – it's etched into the lines of her face.

27

I'm about to thank Giulio for the ride as we pull up outside Nina's bar, my plan being to throw myself on my bed and spill all to Isla before we open up again. But before I can even open my mouth, he reaches for my hand and gently tugs me down the street. 'It's Sunday, remember? We need gelato ... it's the law.'

A jolt ripples through me at his warm grip, but I brush it off. This is Italy – everyone's touchy-feely, right? I see it all around me. Ren throws his arm around people all the time. It's just ... normal.

But ... my heart doesn't skip a beat when Ren does it.

The streets are quiet and empty, and I suspect everyone in Monti is snoozing off a food coma. There's zero chance of me and Giulio getting separated by crowds of tourists like there was at the Pantheon, but he still holds my hand loosely in his until we find a little gelateria that's open for business during the long hot afternoon hours – a little gelateria that still has about twenty-five different flavours on offer. There are classics like *cioccolato* and *crema*, but also caramelized fig and ricotta, and a purple hyacinth ice cream with real petals in it.

'I'll have to show Ren this place, although he'd probably convince them to make French onion gelato or something,' I joke.

For a second, Giulio's relaxed expression puckers into something like irritation, like it often does when Ren's name comes up.

We each get a cone and walk over to the fountain that will for ever be tainted by Ma and Pa's first kiss – knowledge I'm not about to share with Giulio. We find a spot on the ledge and I leave a decent amount of space between us. But then more people arrive, forcing Giulio to squish up next to me. He's still doing that annoying boy thing, though, where he takes up all the leg room. I nudge the knee invading my space, and he pushes back . . . until we're full-on knee-wrestling. My leg is about a foot shorter and I start to topple backwards. I fling my arm out just in time, waving gelato everywhere, but my hand slips on the edge of the fountain and my arm plunges into the cool water, right up to my elbow.

'Bathing in the works of art . . .' Giulio shakes his head in mock disappointment. 'And I was starting to think you were one of the locals.'

He's leaning back, staring at me ... no, wait ... he's staring at my family heirloom of a nose.

'It's my nose, right?' I blurt, trying to play it off like a joke. 'There's no denying it's Roman.'

His lips twitch as if he's about to tease me, but he doesn't. Instead, he leans in and lifts a hand to my face. My breath catches. *Ommioddio* ... is he going to ... honk it?!

I shrink back, but his hand keeps coming.

'Hold still,' he murmurs, 'you have a blob of gelato right ... there.' His thumb brushes the tip of my nose, slow and deliberate, almost a caress.

'Oh,' I say faintly, my voice barely there.

I'm rooted to the spot, my nose tingling where his thumb had been. How is he so composed when I feel like my heart's about to burst from my chest?

'Yeah, I'm surprised that doesn't happen more often,' I mutter. 'You know, given the size of it.'

Giulio shakes his head with a laugh. 'I like your nose ... it suits your stubborn streak. Another thing that runs in your family.'

I think of Ma and Nina at the hospital, how neither of them backed down, how Ma kept pushing without really saying what she wanted to say.

'Err ... is that supposed to make me feel better?'

'You have nothing to feel bad about,' he says, softly. 'I think it makes you a *tipa*.'

I touch my nose self-consciously. 'Umm . . . I don't know that word. And I'm not sure I want to, either.'

Lies! All lies. I desperately want to know, especially when he's looking at me so . . . so . . .

'It means you're unique in . . .' He hesitates, swallowing hard. 'In an attractive way.'

The air between us crackles and Ma's jokey comment about creating a new first-kiss tradition in this very spot canters through my mind. I push it away, hard, turning to look into the waters behind me.

It's not the Trevi Fountain, but there are still a few coins glittering at the bottom, their surfaces catching the sunlight.

'Ready to go back?' Giulio offers me a hand to pull me to my feet and, as I stand, I wonder what I would wish for if I threw in a coin. Not a kiss, obviously. Definitely not. Probably for the bar to be saved, for Ma and Nina to stop fighting. And for everything to just . . . work out.

28

'Start talking, Livia. I want to hear all about your little sightseeing trip.'

As soon as I walk into class on Monday afternoon, it's glaringly obvious why Kenzi asked me and the others to come early.

'He just took me to some places Nina showed him,' I say lightly. 'He's actually a pretty good *cicerone*.'

Sofia frowns. 'What's that?'

'Basically, a tour guide,' I explain, feeling a tiny bit proud of myself for knowing this very Italian term. 'But, you know, a fancy Roman one.'

More like a Roman you fancy, Liv . . .

Heat creeps up my neck as Inner Isla's comment hits its mark.

Kenzi, Ren and Sofia exchange loaded glances. It's clear they're not going to let this go so easily.

'He just took me to some places Nina showed him,' I repeat, as if it was no big deal. As if I haven't been reliving every minute of it – wandering through Nina's favourite spots, seeing Rome from a completely different angle. It felt like some kind of fusion tourism, like Ren's cooking – mixing the big, touristy sights with the hidden, local way of seeing them. Familiar, but new. Even the framed poster of St Peter's sends me right back to that keyhole, and how small and perfect it looked.

'Wait, wait, wait.' Sofia's voice cuts through my thoughts. 'Are you saying you've finally succumbed to Giulio's charm?'

'No! He's just . . . I don't know, easier to talk to than I expected.'

Ren pokes a finger into my ribs. 'Easier to talk to? Or easier to look at?'

'*Vi prego*, enough!' I beg.

Sofia grins. 'Just trying to understand if Giulio's one of us now.'

'I wouldn't go that far,' I say. 'It's more because . . .' I take a deep breath and tell my friends everything they've missed: Nina trying to convince Giulio to spy on Ma, the mountain of debt we have a week to pay back, and how we might lose the bar just when I'm finally – *finally* – starting to feel like I belong.

The shock doesn't leave their faces. Ugh! I've totally killed the mood.

'What about you, Ren? How was the tour?' I'm counting on his love of food to lighten the mood, but he doesn't take the bait.

'It was great. We took loads of photos. But, Livia, we should talk about your situation.'

I turn to Kenzi to ask about her weekend, but she stops me just as I take a breath.

'I helped Mehdi with his citizenship paperwork. Now, back to you. What are you going to do about the bar?'

I rest my head in my hands. 'It's . . . complicated. The debts are worse than I thought. Giulio's even thinking about selling his Vespa to help cover it. And Ma doesn't know a thing.'

Sofia bites her lip. 'But the bar's been busier, no?'

'*Sì*,' I nod. 'Giulio says it's not enough to impress the bank, but . . . I don't know.'

Kenzi's eyes light up with an idea. 'Then let's make it enough. What if we open up the language swap to more people?'

'Who would come? How do we get more people interested?' I ask.

Sofia waves her phone. 'I could mention it on my travel blog and social media feeds. My followers would love it, especially if they get free conversation practice.'

'I could make snacks,' Ren says. 'Everyone loves free food, right?'

'I suppose . . .' I start, but Kenzi's nodding.

'We're already doing it . . . we just need to go—'

'Bigger!' I finish, a stirring of hope warming my insides for the first time in days. 'We could make it a regular thing . . .'

My heart races. This could actually work.

29

My new friends are actual legends. Knowing how desperate the situation has become, they pulled out all the stops to get our new open-to-all language swap up and running the very next day. We've barely finished setting up, and there's already a steady trickle of people coming into the bar.

Giulio wasn't exactly thrilled at the idea, but since he's already admitted the bar needs more than just a busy Sunday to survive, he hasn't stood in our way. He is, however, standing at the counter with his arms folded and eyes narrowed, watching Ren move around the tables with a platter of bite-sized seaweed parmesan gougères – French cheese puffs made with Japanese nori and Italian parmesan.

'You forgot to put something English, Portuguese and Arabic into the mix, too.'

There's an unmistakable challenge in Giulio's voice as he points to the *six* language tables we've set up around the bar. But that only reminds me how proud I am that the four of us have come up with six languages between us. For once, it feels like we have something to offer instead of something to make up for.

It's Sofia's efforts that have drawn in the crowd, though. She's been posting regular updates on her blog and social media, and Kenzi made flyers using the language school's computers and photocopier, thanks to Mas-si turning a blind eye.

Ma's reaction has been harder to read. She hasn't said much at all, which is SO unlike her. It makes me wonder if, deep down, she'd prefer it if the bar closed and forced Nina into retirement. Or maybe she's worried about how Nina will cope if things do get busier. Maybe it's both, because she definitely looked torn. And, well, I'm too nervous to ask her and find out.

It's a while before I have time to check in with Giulio.

I raise one eyebrow – *What do you think?*

He quirks one in return – *Not sure. Could work.*

I respond with a slight frown and a head tilt – *Is it enough, though?*

He does what I can only describe as an eyebrow shrug – *Maybe.*

And then Signora Pedretti's tugging his arm and holding up her phone. 'Flaminia's VideoFacing me, but she can't see me.'

'You did this last time, too. Thumb off the camera, Signora.' Giulio's tone is half amusement, half exasperation. He leans in next to Signora Pedretti and grins at the screen. 'If I have to manage every call like this, you might as well ring me directly,' he jokes, earning a giggle from Flaminia.

Kenzi laughs too as she surveys the scene. But then she catches my expression and goes quiet, her eyes searching mine as if she's seeing something I'm not ready to admit.

'Are you . . . OK?' she asks hesitantly. 'It's just, Mehdi's going to kill me if I stay more than an hour. My parents are out tonight and he's stuck babysitting again, but I don't want to leave if—'

I lay a hand on her forearm, stopping her. 'I'm fine. Go when you need to . . . or get your brother to come along,' I say, forcing a brightness I don't feel into my voice.

Kenzi shakes her head. 'He has to go and see a friend about a potential job. But this is looking promising, right? And look, we haven't scared the regulars away either.'

She's right. Enrico has drifted away from the snack table and is now approaching us with an older lady I've never seen before. The woman says something to Kenzi in what I assume is Arabic, her tone warm and friendly. I don't understand a word, but from the way Kenzi's shoulders lift in a modest shrug and her hands wave dismissively, as if to say 'no need to thank me', it must be about the prescription she helped translate a few weeks ago.

As the woman moves away, Kenzi leans in slightly. 'Mehdi might not come, but I could bring my jad one night. He'd love this – he's always looking for someone other than my family to talk to.'

Something warm unfurls inside me, even as my thoughts catch briefly on Giulio and Flaminia and their easy laughter. It's moments like these that make the bar more than just a place to grab a coffee. It's a little community, where people can help each other, connect over languages and find common ground. Here, it's like everyone belongs.

We close much later than usual, and I'm yawning as I settle into the rooftop hammock to FaceTime Isla. It's dark here in Rome – well, as dark as it gets when there's light pollution – but the cattery is bathed in the pale evening light of a northern summer. Isla is sprawled on the sofa, surrounded by a *glaring* of cats – an accurate collective noun, given how they excel at silently judging everyone.

'You look like a Bond villain.'

'Really?' Isla perks up. 'That's actually the look I was going for.'

'Why does that not surprise me? So . . . how are things in Edinburgh?' I ask, hoping to avoid her usual interrogation.

'Let's see . . . It's cold and raining, obviously. I'm here for the night while your dad is away living the life at a wedding. My new hoodie is covered in cat hair and my best friend is – what was it? – 1,500 miles away? You'd better have something juicy to tell me Livia Nardelli, because I am living through you now.'

I try to bring her up to speed with the language swap, but she interrupts me.

'No. By juicy, I mean something tall, dark and Giulio. Your mum said you were out all afternoon the other day . . . alone . . . together.'

A noise at my back makes my blood run cold. Giulio's stepping over the railing to my side of the terrace. Oh no. Did he hear Isla?

'Wait . . . your face!' Isla shoots upright on the sofa, sending cats scurrying in all directions. 'He's there, isn't he?'

I react so fast I practically tip myself out of the hammock and land in a heap on the terrace. I pick myself up, my voice low and urgent. 'Isla, no—'

'Oh my God, Liv. Don't be selfish. Let me see the

hot Italian boy again!'

'*Ommioddio*,' I groan, mortified in more ways than I can count. 'You're turning into Ma. This has to stop.'

Ignoring me, she shouts, 'Hi, Giulio! Nice to meet you!'

My entire nervous system short-circuits when Giulio leans into the frame, half-laughing. '*Ciao*, Isla!'

Isla places the back of her hand to her forehead and pretends to swoon. 'Say my name again!'

Yup. Isla is definitely a villain.

'I'm hanging up now!' I say, turning my phone off quickly because, while I can't think of anything worse happening right now, I bet Isla could surprise me. I smile weakly at Giulio. 'Sorry about that.'

He leans against the balustrade, an amused grin lifting one side of his mouth. Then his expression shifts, his eyes darkening. 'I thought I'd find you out here.'

My heart loop the loops. He came looking for me? The person he finds . . . unique, in an attractive way?

'We should talk about the swap,' he says, casually. 'See how much we made today.'

'*Sì, certo*.' I try to sound nonchalant while my stomach sinks a little. I mentally scold myself for being ridiculous. Obviously he's here to talk business. What else would he need me for? 'So, how did we do?'

He scrolls through some numbers on his phone.

'We made just under four hundred euros. Better than Sunday morning . . . but even if this keeps up, we'd never pay off the debt in time – even with the Vespa as a down payment.'

I chew the inside of my cheek. 'How much is it worth?'

He pauses, then sighs. 'A vintage Vespa, in good condition? Around seven thousand, maybe more. Bertolli's only offering five.'

I frown. Bertolli clearly knows Giulio's in a difficult position and is taking advantage. I do a quick mental calculation. Even with today's earnings, it would take too long to make that money – and that's without taking the rest of the debt into account, or the bills and overheads and all the other things Ma's been muttering about. I feel silly for getting my hopes up earlier – as if a bunch of teens can really make a difference.

'Five thousand . . .' I repeat, my voice trailing off. 'That's a lot.'

Giulio leans back against the wall, crossing his arms. 'And the bank isn't going to wait for ever.'

I force myself to focus. 'What if . . . we trial the swap for another day or two and, if it carries on like this, we invite Bertolli to see for himself? He might give us more time if he thinks business is picking up.'

He considers it. 'You think?'

I warm to the idea. 'If we show him there's potential for real, long-term change, he might. But . . .' I check over my shoulder, making sure we're alone. 'We'll have to keep it from Ma somehow.'

Giulio lets out a long sigh. 'It's worth a try, I suppose.'

As he goes back on his phone, I catch myself staring at him for a moment too long. Why did I even think for a second he came to see me? I shake my head, reminding myself to stay focused. It's just the bar, the Vespa, the debt.

Besides, even if there was something more, Ma would go into overdrive. All the progress I've made at fitting in would be gone in a blink. I can practically hear her voice now: *Another foreign girl bites the dust*.

30

The language swap gets busier with each passing day, and today is the busiest yet. Laughter and languages fill the air. I even overhear Enrico teaching a French tourist the art of creative insults – something modern-day Romans are renowned for all over Italy.

I'm tempted to join in, but I can barely drag my eyes away from the entrance. Giulio has been begging Bertolli to come and see our initiative, and, with only two days to convince him the bar's an investment worth saving, I'm both relieved and terrified he's finally agreed.

Giulio's as tense as I am, his head snapping up every time someone new arrives. Our mission: intercept Bertolli before Ma sees him. The idea – a flimsy one – is to hide him in plain sight, but we'll only be able to do that if he comes now while the bar is busy. And more importantly, he needs to *see* it's busy if we're going to convince him to give us more time.

I tell myself he'll be there on the count of ten, but

I'm only at eight when a shadow moves in the doorway. It's him – Bertolli. He's stopped on the threshold as if his gaze has caught on something. Following his line of sight, I see it – Giulio's Vespa, parked by the entrance. His greedy eyes roam over the bike like it's already his.

'Here we go,' Giulio mutters before putting on his best smile and going to greet him.

Bertolli strolls around the bar, hands clasped behind his back, pale grey eyes sliding over every detail – inspecting, weighing . . . calculating. He reminds me of a briefcase, all leathery and square-angled, full of importance. It's clear he's not here for the swap, and my eyes dart nervously to Ma. She's stuck behind the counter, serving customers, but she's craning her neck, like she wants to know who I'm talking to and is frustrated she can't see properly. Weirdly, Bertolli always seems to have his back to her, as if he's just as keen to avoid her as we are.

'*Interessante* . . .' Bertolli circles back to the entrance where Giulio and I are waiting for him, as far from the counter as possible. 'I see the potential, I really do . . .'

Hope sparks in my veins. Maybe this will work. Maybe he'll see we're making real progress. I force a smile. 'We're hoping this will really turn the business around.'

Bertolli wets his lips, eyes straying once more to the Vespa. 'But potential does not pay off debts. If you had not already missed a number of payments . . . perhaps. But the terms of our agreement have been breached.'

Giulio shifts beside me. 'We just need a bit more time.'

I clench my fists at my sides, my thoughts spinning as I try to come up with a convincing argument.

Bertolli's voice cuts through the noise in my head, calm and unbothered. 'If I have the Vespa as a down payment, that will give you time to get established.'

My heart sinks. Giulio's standing rigid, his jaw locked tight. I can't let this happen. I step forward, my voice shaky but determined. 'It was his nonna's . . . It has sentimental value. What if we sold something else?'

Bertolli eyes me with cold indifference. 'Only the Vespa. Or seven thousand euros. You have three days left.'

'But you said it was worth five!' Giulio exclaims, then he hushes, looking to see if Ma noticed. 'You can't.'

My skin crawls at the snake-flicker of Bertolli's tongue. 'Five is what I'm willing to pay, to help you out of this fix. But if you do not need my help, then seven is what you need to come up with.'

It's clear he's not interested in saving the bar. He

doesn't care if we make it or not. All he wants is the Vespa, and he's just biding his time, knowing we're running out of options.

Bertolli dismisses us, even though he's the one leaving, and Signora Pedretti sidles over, scowling at his retreating figure.

'I know that man,' she says quietly. 'He forced Enrico and his wife to close their trattoria. And that's not all.' She bites her lip as if debating whether to say more, then shakes her head. 'Just watch yourselves with that one, OK?'

31

'Livia Nardelli. What is going on here?'

Uh-oh. Ma's tone. My full name delivered in the same voice my PE teacher used when she caught me and Isla sneaking a Snickers behind the bus shelter instead of taking the proper route on the cross-country run. That sinking feeling in my gut is the same, too. Only this time, I'm eating one of Ren's Chantilly cream cannoli instead of a chocolate bar.

'Why was that man here?' Ma beams her eye lasers at me and it's like she can see the secrets I've crammed inside.

'Man?' I play for time, pretending the word is foreign to me, one I've never heard in English or Italian.

Ma inhales through her nose. Loudly. Slowly. '*Sì*, Livia. The one who was looking around the bar as if it belonged to him.'

I gulp. She has no idea how close to the truth that is.

Giulio's micro-frown begs me to keep quiet, but I can't. I can't lie to her any more. Not when Bertolli has just taken away any hope we had of fixing this ourselves.

'He's from the bank. His name is Bertolli.' I draw a deep breath like I've finally taken off something too tight. 'And the bar is in debt. Badly in debt.'

For a moment, Ma just stares, and my stomach churns.

'We didn't want to worry you,' I continue, my voice quieter now. 'You've already got so much going on with Nina . . .'

'What debt?' Ma puffs up like an angry cat; her words hiss. 'You've been here for . . . what? Four weeks? And you think you run this place? That you know everything? That you can keep something like this from me?'

Her words land like a slap. Four weeks. Like that's all I am – as if everything I've been doing, everything I've been trying to prove, can just be brushed off.

Like I don't really belong here.

'And you're sure Bertolli's a bank manager, *sì*?' Ma searches my face. 'You're sure he isn't . . . something else?'

I shake my head, half in answer, half in confusion. Why is she asking me that?

Giulio steps forward. 'Livia wanted to tell you . . . but—'

Ma spins on him. 'This is Nina's doing, isn't it? She told you not to trust me.'

'No!' I clutch Ma's arm. 'Nina doesn't know either. I mean . . . she knows about the loan, obviously. But she doesn't know Bertolli's demanding settlement. And the only reason I didn't tell you immediately is that I didn't want this to be *another* thing for you two to argue about!'

I practically shouted that last bit. Out of the corner of my eye, Kenzi tries to catch my attention, her face saying – *everything OK?* And Sofia and Ren look ready to jump out of their seats to back me up.

Ma opens her mouth, but I'm on a roll now.

'You've been so weird about the language swap . . . like you're not happy business has picked up . . . like you want the bar to fail. I wasn't sure you'd be on our side.'

Ma gawps at me like a landed fish.

Signora Pedretti, who has been unashamedly listening in, rests a comforting hand on Ma's back. 'Livia has a point, Caterina. You asked me to gauge how Adelina feels about retiring. You've been torn about this bar's future for a while now.'

Ma's jaw clenches. When she speaks, her voice is barely audible, but I hear the hurt in it. 'I should've been told.'

A quiet settles over us, with just the chatter of the language swap to mask the tension. Ma takes a deep breath, then slowly exhales. 'I need to know everything. No more secrets.' Her eyes move between Giulio and me. 'And you two are coming with me to the hospital tomorrow.'

32

Ma video-calls Pa the minute we lock up and I'm forced to endure a joint telling-off before I make my escape to the roof terrace. But I have another reason for being up here. I cross to Giulio's side, practising my apology in my head as I knock on his door and wait for the sound of his footsteps. But the silence stretches on. Is he so angry I blabbed to Ma, that he won't even talk to me now?

That's when I hear it – a familiar drawl behind me.

'Looking for me, Scotland?'

I spin around, blinking in surprise, to find Giulio lounging in the hammock. 'Wait – have you been there this whole time, just letting me knock like an idiot?'

'It's my hammock . . . where else would I be?' His legs are so long he can push off the balustrade with his feet to make it sway.

'Yours?' I point to the railing dividing the terraces. 'But it's on Nina's side.' As soon as I say the words, they sound ridiculous even to my own ears. I can't imagine Nina relaxing there ... or anywhere. Ever.

Giulio sits up, balancing easily, and I envy his irritatingly effortless grace. 'It's sunnier here in spring,' he explains. 'By summer, though, it's cooler on my side.' The corner of his mouth hitches up as he adds, 'I was going to move it back, but this annoying girl showed up. She was so ... *stressata*, I figured she needed it more than I did.'

I plant my hands on my hips in mock outrage, but I'm working hard to hide my own smile. He's teasing me ... and if he's teasing me, he can't be angry. My relief is ... is ...

Telling? Inner Isla supplies in a dry voice.

'Did it ever occur to you,' I counter, 'that *you* were the one stressing this poor girl out?'

'Me? I'm too much of a *gentiluomo* to ever do that.' His grin is bright in the darkness, but it's definitely not gentlemanly. Especially when he shifts and pats the spot beside him. 'Look ... I'm even willing to share.'

I hesitate for a second. Inner Isla snorts. *You share so much already – the bar, Nina's troubles, her favourite Roman hotspots. Go right ahead. I would.*

I sing a little tra-la-la in my head to drown her out and attempt to sit back into the hammock, smooth and Giulio-style ... but it shifts and rocks beneath me.

I shoot a suspiciously blank-faced Giulio an accusing glare. 'You're doing that on purpose!'

I grab hold as it lurches sideways, my arms windmilling, my legs flailing for balance.

And then Giulio's arms wrap around me, pulling me to him. Steadying us both.

We are close.

Awkwardly close.

Closer than on the Vespa. And this time, we're face to face – our breath mingling in the few centimetres separating my mouth from his. And I seem to have developed an extra sense – one that is purely for him.

'Comfy, Scotland?'

Hardly. The whisper of his words sends goosebumps up my spine and, *ommioddio*, I don't think I've ever felt *less* comfortable in my life. My heart is pounding in my chest, my throat . . . even in my fingertips.

He watches with an amused smirk and I scramble for something to say. Anything at all.

'I'm sorry I told Ma.'

Agh! No! Not that!

Giulio looks up at the dark haze of the sky. 'It had to come out sooner or later.'

'I suppose.'

'And maybe your mum will have some other ideas

we can use along with the Vespa.'

My hand hovers over his forearm, not daring to touch him. 'You heard Signora Pedretti. She said not to do any deals with Bertolli . . . that he can't be trusted.'

Giulio's big brown cow eyes are serious for once. 'I could never enjoy it again. Not if Nina loses the bar just because I wanted to keep it. I know you think she's not my family . . .'

I cringe at the memory and dip my chin, not realizing there's so little space I've practically buried my face in his chest. I jerk my head up again and take a deep breath. 'Look, I'm sorry I said that. I get it now. I was . . . jealous. I've been away for so long and . . . I felt like you were taking my place.'

Oddly, I'm more relieved than embarrassed by my confession. Today is a day for truths.

Giulio's soft laugh stirs the frizzy strands of hair around my face. 'And I thought you would take mine.'

I blink. 'Me, take Golden Boy Giulio's place? That's ridiculous!'

He fake-scowls at the nickname. '*Davvero?* Is it? Because I was worried she'd be so happy to finally have her *actual* granddaughter here, she wouldn't need me any more.'

My lips part in disbelief. We'd both been thinking the same thing all along, worrying we'd taken up too much space in the other's life. It's as if I'm seeing a whole new side to him, a side that understands exactly where I've been coming from, a side that sees the real me.

'And how do you feel now?' OK. I really wish I'd worded that differently ... and that my voice wasn't so breathy. And did my body really strain towards him without my say-so?

The hammock is perfectly still now, but everything around us feels like it's tipping ... waiting. It's just us, balancing between the old and new understanding we have of each other.

'Now ...' Giulio's lips are a mere whisper from mine ... brushing them as he murmurs. 'Now I feel ...'

'Livia!'

Ma calls up from the bottom of the stairs and Giulio and I startle like a jump scare in a horror film. The hammock rocks wildly and ...

'Uh-oh!' Giulio's eyes widen.

Before either of us can stop it, we tip right over, crashing on to the terrace floor in a jumble of limbs and heavy fabric. My elbow jabs into his side, and I groan as his chin bumps against the top of my head.

We untangle ourselves, red-faced but grinning like idiots.

'Ma has impeccable timing,' I mutter, half embarrassed, half exasperated, as she calls again, asking if I've seen her favourite cat pyjamas anywhere.

If only she knew what she just interrupted.

33

I can't think about my rooftop rendezvous with Giulio last night without my face bursting into flames. But I can't *stop* thinking about it either — which basically means my cheeks have been on fire non-stop. So when Giulio walks into the bar the next morning, I immediately insert my head into the under-counter fridge.

'So, umm, I'm not sure we have enough milk, but . . . do we increase the order, cancel it completely or keep it as it is?'

There. Cool and professional and not at all flustered about our near-kiss last night.

But it's Ma who answers. 'Don't place any orders, Livia, *d'accordo?*'

I pull my head out to find Ma looking smarter than I've ever seen her — so put together, I suspect she's raided Nina's wardrobe, because even Nina's dressing gowns have a tailored look about them. And the reason she's sneaked up so soundlessly is not because she was a cat in her former life, but because she's barefoot — a pair of heeled sandals from the rack upstairs dangling from her fingertips.

I point to the few remaining milk cartons. 'But it's been busy—'

'And we have no idea if the bar will still be ours after tomorrow,' she finishes.

Uff! The words land like a gut punch as Ma reaches over to close the fridge door. Not that I need it any more. I've gone cold all over. We've come so far, worked so hard to turn the bar around . . . how has it got to the point where there's no point ordering milk?

Ma hikes a smart leather handbag — also not hers — on to her shoulder. 'I've got things to do this morning, but can you two pick up some food and meet me outside the hospital at 1 p.m.?' Her gaze locks with mine. 'Outside, *d'accordo*? No sneaking in to talk to Nina without me.'

We both give Ma a silent nod.

She puts on the sandals and totters out of the bar. Giulio and I watch until she disappears from sight, pausing every few paces to free the stiletto heel from the pavement cracks.

We're focused so intently that we both jump when a loud meow suddenly echoes through the bar.

Giulio's head whips round. 'Is there a cat in here?'

'Nope ... that's Ma's ringtone. She must've left her phone.' I scan the counter and spot it peeping out from under the pile of daily newspapers that were delivered a short while ago.

A notification lights up the screen and my heart jumps into my throat. 'It's a message from Bertolli.'

'*Cosa?* What does it say?' Giulio's beside me in a second.

I type in Ma's Password-For-Everything and read the short text. 'It's instructions on how to access his office building. And look at this ...' I show Giulio the screen.

It will be a pleasure doing business with you again.

I frown up at Giulio. 'Again? Does Ma know Bertolli?'

Giulio rubs a hand down his face and groans. 'This is exactly what Nina was worried about ... Caterina having secret meetings.'

The minutes drag after that, the clock hands barely moving, even with the bar getting busier around us.

Now, as we sit outside the hospital, it's still the same.

The parmigiana we picked up for Nina is balanced on Giulio's knee, bouncing in time to his jitters. I can only imagine what kind of mess it'll be in when she opens the container – a lumpy disaster of aubergine and mozzarella. The last thing we need is a ruined lunch on top of the bad news we're about to deliver.

I try to read Ma's face as she hobbles across the small piazza, her panda-eyed look of exhaustion saying more than she ever could. Whatever happened with Bertolli, it can't be good.

But first things first.

I pull her phone from my pocket and thrust it towards her. 'We know you've been to see Bertolli.'

Ma actually looks around as if something might swoop in to save her from answering, then she presses her lips into a line. 'Fine. But can we go inside? I'd rather say what I have to say only once.'

Nina is sitting upright today, and her leg – which had been suspended in a sling during our last visit – is now free, although wrapped in a cast from her ankle to her knee. And there's a wheelchair in the corner of the room, ready for use.

Nina frowns at Ma – their standard mother–daughter greeting. 'What are you doing here on a weekday, Caterina?'

Ma looks like she's about to pull a wax strip off her upper lip. She's going for the quick-rip method too, because she cuts right to the chase. 'I've been to see Bertolli.'

Nina pales, her blushed cheekbones clownish

against her papery skin. 'Caterina . . . you didn't. Not again . . .'

Giulio and I exchange eyebrow messages over her head. *Not again? What does that mean?*

Ma clears her throat. 'Your loan—'

'Is my business,' Nina interrupts. 'Have you been snooping in my private papers?'

'No, Mamma, you've got it wrong. Bertolli's overseeing your loan. He works for the bank now.'

'What? No. He's a property developer. How can he be with the bank?' A tiny furrow appears between Nina's brows. She must be frowning hard.

'The previous manager retired last month,' Ma explains. 'Bertolli was hired and he's the one in charge now, Mamma.'

Nina looks stunned. 'And you didn't think to tell me this sooner?'

Ma spreads her hands wide. 'I didn't know any of it until yesterday . . . I didn't even know you'd borrowed that money! Why didn't you tell me?'

'And hear you say I told you so? That I couldn't manage? That I was past it?' Nina folds her arms across her chest, looking old and toddler-like at the same time.

'Well . . . you have fallen behind on the payments, Mamma. Three months' worth.'

'So?' Nina shrugs. 'I've been late before. They know I'm good for it.'

'This time is different,' Ma says softly. 'Bertolli pointed out a fine-print clause in the contract. He's demanding the full balance – fifteen thousand euros – or . . .'

Nina sets her jaw. 'Or what?'

Ma waits for Nina to look at her. 'Or he's going to repossess the bar. And the apartment too. The whole property's tied up in the loan, Mamma. And I think he's been slyly waiting for time to run out . . . hiding from you . . . from me . . .'

Nina's expression darkens. 'He's always wanted that bar. Always . . .' Her voice trails off and, whatever she's remembering, it isn't pleasant.

'He said he'd take five thousand euros from the debt if I give him my Vespa.'

I've been so focused on Ma and Nina, and the volley of words passing between them, that I'd forgotten Giulio was here . . . *Cavolo!* I'd almost forgotten *I* was here.

Nina snaps back to the present. 'Over my dead body! You are not giving him that Vespa. And let's be clear – I'm very much alive.' The Vespa issue is dismissed just like that. 'So, what did you arrange with him this time, Caterina?'

Right. That's it. I am fed up of secrets.

'What do you mean this time?' I burst out. 'We should be working together ... but how can we, when none of us has the full picture? What's going on?' My trainers squeak on the tiled floor as I swivel to face Ma. 'And how do you know Bertolli?'

Nina lifts her chin, her piercing gaze never leaving Ma. 'Go on, Caterina. Tell her.'

34

Ma slumps on to the plastic visitor's chair, her legs sticking out in front of her like a doll's. 'Ten years ago . . . I looked into selling the bar.'

Giulio and I gasp. The bar is everything to Nina. It's all she talks about. It's her way of life, not just a job . . . and now, having worked there, I understand it in a way I never could before. It's family, it's history, it's identity . . . it's our piece of Rome.

What was Ma thinking?

'Oh, it was a bit more than that, Caterina,' Nina says coldly. 'You and Bertolli had the contract all ready for me to sign.'

I think of the slimy way Bertolli prowled around the bar at the language swap. He doesn't just want the Vespa. He wants the whole thing.

'The bar was in bad shape,' Ma protests. 'You have to adm—'

'You mean *I* was in bad shape,' Nina cuts her off. 'Just because I'd reached retirement age. That's what hurt me the most, Caterina.'

'That's not true, Mamma.' Ma clutches her forehead, as if to stop the memories resurfacing. 'I didn't know what else to do. The bar was struggling. I'd moved away to Scotland, but I felt guilty every single day for leaving. And then Bertolli – he made it sound like you would still manage it, that he just wanted to turn it around.'

Nina doesn't speak when Ma pauses for breath, but her stillness and the fact she's not interrupting like she usually does gives Ma that extra bit of courage to carry on.

'I've been trying to tell you I was wrong for years. I thought I was doing it for you ... but the truth is I wanted you with me. I thought if you weren't so tied up with the bar, you could spend time with us ... in Scotland.' Ma's voice cracks then, and I see into it, to the pain of the past, how much she's missed having Nina in her life.

Nina doesn't look up, but there's a shift – a softening in her tough exterior. 'Well, Caterina ... if Bertolli is serious about repossessing the bar ... that may well happen.'

'But we have to stop him!' I look at the faces around me, each one tense and strained. 'We can't let him win. Not when the bar's doing so well. You should see it, Nina. We've started up a language swap and it's really taken off.'

Nina's eyes find mine. 'And my customers? Bringing in new people is one thing, but are they scaring away the regulars? Are these changes pushing out the people who've kept this place alive for years?'

The chill in her voice makes me hesitate, but I push through. 'We didn't set out to change too much. But I really think it's been helping.'

'They are enjoying it. Enrico has been in every evening, too, not just for breakfast.' Giulio's fingers brush the back of my hand and I don't think it's accidental. He's letting me know he's there . . . for me. A few weeks ago, he might've agreed with Nina, that I didn't understand the bar or its history. But now . . . now he's on my side. We're a team.

Nina's expression softens slightly, but the protectiveness is still there. 'I appreciate the effort, Livia. I do. But don't forget what the bar means, and who it's meant for. I don't want it turning into a fancy drinks venue that doesn't value loyal customers. And if Bertolli gets his hands on it, that's exactly what it will become.'

35

Ma leaves to consult an old lawyer friend to see if there are any legal loopholes we can grab on to, so Giulio and I head back alone. Only instead of taking the usual route to the bar, he parks the Vespa along the riverside instead.

'*Vieni!*' He slides off the saddle and beckons for me to do the same. 'We still have an hour to kill before reopening, no point sitting about worrying until Caterina gets back.'

I blink, caught off guard. 'You want to go somewhere ... now?'

'Got any better ideas?' He does that loose Italian shrug I can never quite pull off.

Yes, but Giulio has SHOULDERS – I actually hear the capitals in Inner Isla's voice.

I walk beside him through the narrow streets – because I'm curious, not because he has great shoulders – until we spill out into Piazza Navona. I recognize it instantly – from the postcards on the revolving stands outside the tourist shops, and the huge poster on the wall of the language school classroom. But seeing it in real life still takes my breath away – the huge fountains drawing people to them like magnets, the beautiful buildings hugging the perimeter. There are street artists and performers, market stalls and music. There's something about the atmosphere too, like I've been here before, but not only as a six-year-old child.

My stomach churns. Will we ever come back to Rome if we lose the bar? And would we stay in a hotel like we're visitors just passing through . . . or with Nina in some unfamiliar suburb? And what about Giulio? He'd be losing more than a job. He'd lose everything that grounds him; the stability Nina has given him over the years.

He tugs the end of my ponytail, pulling my attention back to the beautiful piazza. 'You OK?'

'*Sì*, just . . . thinking.' I fidget with the strap of my tank top and he slips an arm around my shoulders, tucking me into his side.

My ability to coordinate my feet goes wonky and we bump hips awkwardly for a few steps. I think we're heading for the main attraction – the Fountain of the Four Rivers – with its muscly statues representing different continents. I mean, this thing even has an obelisk sticking out of it. But Giulio steers us down a side street instead. A few turns later, we stop in front of . . . a broken statue? I eye the crumbling torso and its vague face – my brain sifting through all the Roman trivia Ma's spouted over the years. And come up blank.

Giulio bows. 'Livia, meet Pasquino. Pasquino, *ti presento*, Livia.'

I fold my arms and shift my weight on to one leg. 'You think some old statue is going to cheer us up? Save the bar?'

'Pasquino isn't any old statue. He's a talking statue.'

'Aaand?' I make a rolling motion with my hand, inviting him to keep talking until he makes sense.

'Think of him as the comments section on social media.'

'Nope. Still nothing.'

He points to the base of the statue, and the scraps of paper crammed into its cracks and even stuck on with . . . urgh . . . chewing gum.

'This is where the little people come when they have no voice of their own. Notes, protests, complaints – especially about those in power . . . Romans have been doing it for centuries. In fact, I bet a few of those are Nina's.'

'Wait – this is one of her spots?' I look closer at the jumble of notes.

One reads: *Politicians line their pockets while we struggle to pay our rent.*

Another declares: *The buses are never on time! How can we work when public transport fails us?* Underneath, someone's drawn an angry face, and another has taped a notice of a transport strike tomorrow.

'Wow,' I murmur. 'It really is like an ancient social media feed.'

Giulio points to a bright yellow note taped to the other side of the base. 'Hey, why didn't you tell me you'd been here already?'

I blink. 'What? I haven't.'

He taps the note and I peer in to read it.

I fell for you, but I didn't tell you. And now it's too late.

That stomach flip evolves into a full-on somersault and I let out a tiny squeak.

'Looks like someone's mistaken old Pasquino here for Cupid,' Giulio jokes. 'Although . . . I suppose we both fell last night. And it's not too late.'

Ommioddio. He's talking about last night. He's *actually* bringing it up. I can almost feel my cheeks turning scarlet and have to resist the urge to dash over to the Fountain of the Four Rivers to plunge my head in it.

But as much as I want to disappear into the ground, I'm just as desperate for him to say more. I freeze, waiting – still crouched, my big nose a mere centimetre away from the note, like I'm a pointer dog drawing attention to it.

Then Giulio's phone buzzes in his pocket. '*Pronto?*'

A girl's voice floats faintly from the speaker, just loud enough to make my breath catch. And while it's over thirty-five degrees outside, a chill chases through me when Giulio takes a few steps away.

And just like that, whatever spell I was under breaks. I pretend to study Pasquino and the notes. But the only letters I can make out are the ones spelling the name on his phone screen – Flaminia.

36

Ma bulldozes me to my language class in the afternoon, desperate to get rid of me and my 'incessant questions'. But when her lawyer friend wasn't able to find a loophole and Pa confirmed he can't free up any savings in time, the idea of having pretend conversations about giving directions and ordering taxis feels . . . as pointless as ordering milk for a bar that's about to be repossessed.

Ma practically hands me over to Kenzi at the school entrance and disappears around the corner at lightning speed.

'What happened at the swap last night? Your mum looked angry . . . did she find out about the debts?'

Was that only last night? So much has happened in so little time. I take a long breath and, as we slowly climb the stairs, I tell Kenzi the short version of the fallout from Bertolli's visit, and the hospital showdown between Ma and Nina.

When we reach the second floor, Kenzi stops to hug me. 'Sounds intense. But things are finally out in the open now, right?'

I nod into her shoulder and spot Mas-si watching us from the classroom doorway. 'You two – ' He stabs a finger at Kenzi and me – 'fourth floor, *immediatamente*.'

Uffa. What now? I straighten up and look at Mas-si. 'Umm, have we done something wrong?'

He drops the serious face in an instant, clearly incapable of keeping up an act despite his love of drama. 'The advanced teacher is back and you two have been promoted. Congratulations!'

'*Evviva!* More Italian classes.' Kenzi slow claps, her voice flat and sarcastic but Mas-si, oblivious, shoos us up to the fourth floor like a proud father.

I notice it though. And I feel for her. I know it annoys her – being seen as Moroccan first, even though she was born and raised here. Frustrating though it is, she has little choice if it will boost her chance of getting citizenship.

'Just think,' I joke. 'It's only for a few more weeks, then you'll be back at school.' But it's a jolting reminder that I'll be gone too. Back to Scotland. Back to Isla. And away from Kenzi, who has become a bigger part of my life than I ever expected.

She swats my arm. '*Grazie mille*, Livia. That really cheers me up.'

I laugh to mask the ache in my chest. But the sound dies in my throat when we reach the top floor. From this height, I get a perfect view of the bar from the stairwell window. And of Giulio standing outside it...

Talking to a girl.

Correction. Laughing with her. A girl in loose jeans and an oversized hoodie, who still manages to look... glossy. She has her back towards me, but I know who she is. And when she turns, there's no mistaking that profile... that perfectly pert little nose...

Flaminia.

My hand grips the banister when I see the helmet in her hands. My anime helmet – at least, the one I've come to think of as mine. She's putting it on... fastening it under her chin.

'You coming?' Kenzi asks, her voice snapping me back to reality.

'Yeah.' I tear my eyes away from the window. But even as we step into the new classroom, the image of Giulio and Flaminia lingers and there's a weird lump in my throat. Is this why she called him at the Pasquino statue? To set up this... date?

The new teacher is waiting for us. She's efficient, no-nonsense, and dives straight into the lesson. And for the first time, I'm actually challenged – and it feels good. The pace is fast and I'm keeping up, even when one horrible, distracting thought just won't leave me alone; Flaminia pressed close to Giulio on the Vespa, feeling the vibration of his laughter through his back – I can picture it so clearly, because I've been there too.

Did I imagine our almost kiss? Am I really just the cliché foreign girl everyone thinks I am?

After class, we pass the window again. My eyes automatically find the bar. No Vespa. No sign of him. Does that mean they're still together?

Sofia and Ren are waiting for us in the stairwell. I swallow hard and force a greeting past the lump in my throat. Ren has a large tote bag filled with Tupperware containers, the corners jutting against the fabric of the bag. Of course. The language swap. With everything that's been going on, I forgot it was on after class.

I chew the inside of my cheek. Is there any point doing it now? I say as much after I bring Ren and Sofia up to speed with the latest developments, but Sofia just scoffs.

'I set up a page for it. People are organizing meet-ups themselves – turns out, that's the beauty of it. The only way to stop it now is to actually close the bar.'

She claps a hand over her mouth, realizing what she's just said.

Kenzi herds us out. 'Hey, the swap is fun. People are enjoying it, and I'm actually improving my English. Even my family seems impressed, which never happens.' She shrugs. 'May as well go out in style, right?'

37

'Looks like we've started up a food swap too.' Kenzi nods to where Enrico has set a tray of *supplì* next to Ren's fusion snacks. The breadcrumb-coated rice balls, filled with melty mozzarella, look crisp and golden as if they've just been fried. My mouth waters as Enrico splits one open, releasing a wisp of steam that curls upwards, spreading its savoury aroma. Ren has outdone himself too, adding pancetta-topped mini quiches and tempura-batter mozzarella sticks with a soy dipping sauce to the table.

People of all ages and backgrounds have gathered to practise their language skills – some for an upcoming holiday, some hoping to connect with family abroad, and others just wanting to meet new people and try something different. But it feels like the end of a fireworks display – one last, bright burst of colour before everything fades to black. And I can't help thinking that image fits me and Giulio too ...

We've gone from being a heartbeat away from sharing a kiss, to being at opposite ends of the bar.

He hasn't looked my way all evening. As soon as he got back, he parked the Vespa and got straight to work. But it's as if his mind is on something – or some*one* – else.

My own thoughts circle back to Pasquino – before Giulio got that phone call, before I saw him with Flaminia.

I fell for you, but I didn't tell you. And now it's too late.

I could have written that misplaced note. Well, not in the same handwriting – Isla says mine looks like I've chucked spaghetti at the page – but the words, they could have been mine. I fell for you. Too late.

Like the bar, I thought we had more time. But he has Flaminia now. She's already going for Vespa rides. Will he take her to meet Nina, too?

I need to know. Even if it hurts. Even if it confirms my fears.

Tomorrow's transport shutdown surfaces in my mind, and I latch on to it.

'I've been thinking about that strike. Should we leave early tomorrow? Traffic will be jammed and you know what Nina's like about lunch.' There. Casual. Not the slightest trace I'm a disaster inside.

'*Sì, lo so* . . . I know, but I might have stuff to do tomorrow.' Giulio fills the portafilter with ground coffee and presses it down, not once meeting my eye.

'Oh.' I pick my heart up off the floor. 'Something important?'

'Just . . . something.' His voice is bland as he concentrates on the four espressos he's making at the same time.

It's been an emotional day already, with all the secrets finally coming out. Now there's a new one. Only maybe this isn't a secret . . . maybe it's just none of my business.

I need a reality check.

And I know exactly where to get it.

It's a few hours before the bar empties and we close for the night, but just seeing Isla's face pop up on the screen drags me out of my slump. Although I am surprised by the backdrop. Instead of the cattery's calming neutral tones, or the clothes piles that 'decorate' Isla's bedroom, there's noise and music and people jostling into her.

I must be frowning because she rolls her eyes. 'Don't tell me you've forgotten what Edinburgh's like at this time of year?'

She flips the camera around to show me a woman juggling fire, hula-hooping and balancing a unicycle on a traffic cone – all at the same time.

'Of course!' I slap the proverbial hand to my

forehead. 'The Fringe Festival!'

Isla's off screen but I hear her mutter, 'AKA a whole month of crowds, chaos and questionable street performances.'

I'd completely forgotten about the arts festival that grips the city centre in August – the street performers, the temporary stages, the people who come from far and wide to see it. But this must be why Piazza Navona felt so familiar today. The buzzing energy, the mix of locals and tourists, the crazy creativity of the performing artists.

Isla's face comes back into view, a smudge of dark lipstick (or chocolate?) across her cheek. 'What's up with you?'

I can tell she's heading for a quieter spot, and I hesitate. 'I can call tomorrow if you're out-out.'

She tips an oversized 'sharing' pack of chocolate buttons towards her mouth. 'I'm battling my way home,' she says around a huge mouthful. 'You can keep me company. Spill.'

I tell her everything – about the language swap's success that's too little too late, and the whole Flaminia situation . . . basically, a double-whammy of failure. '. . . so yeah, maybe Ma's right. I'm just the cliché foreign girl on holiday in Italy, thinking I'm somehow more than that.'

'Aw Liv, I wish I was there right now . . .'

I smile, small and sad, thinking how much I'd like that too.

Then Isla finishes her sentence. 'So I could slap some flipping sense into you.'

Er . . . What?

'Just talk to him,' she groans. 'Or text him or something.'

'I . . . er . . . don't have his number.'

Isla closes her eyes for a long moment. 'Oh Liv, have I taught you nothing?'

'He's always been right here,' I say in my defence. 'At the bar, at the hospital, right next door. I hated it in the beginning, remember? He was always around, always underfoot, like I couldn't escape him even if I tried.'

Wow. I've gone from trying to push him away to desperately wanting him around even more. Now, the thought of him being absent, of him not being part of all this, makes me ache all over like I've got . . . I don't know . . . love flu, or something.

'OK, fine.' Isla sighs dramatically, then grabs two chocolate buttons and sticks them over her eyes. 'Pretend I'm Giulio.' She lowers her voice, putting on an exaggerated Italian accent. 'Livia . . . my love . . . tell me how you feel.'

'*Ommioddio*, you are ridiculous.'

Isla tosses the chocolate buttons in her mouth. 'I'm serious. Just talk to him, Liv. You're not some cliché. You're you. And that's enough.'

Someone in a shiny silver bodysuit with disco-ball antennae approaches Isla with a collection bucket. The screen goes all blurry as she digs out a few coins. But something has just become *very* clear to me.

I might be at a loss when it comes to Giulio, but I know what to do about the bar.

My heart races as the idea forms, piece by piece.

Isla's watching me curiously. 'What's that weird face for?'

'I know how to help the bar. And I only need one day to do it.'

Which is good. Because one day is all we have.

38

The church bells in Rome chime all through the night – on the hour, every hour. I know this because I lie awake, planning and plotting, sending messages, and begging for favours well into the early hours.

But the mistakes I make in the bar the next morning – dropping things and mixing up orders – aren't down to tiredness, or to me being the foreigner who doesn't belong here. No, these come from the nervous energy coursing through me, from the sheer enormity of what we have to do – and how much we stand to lose if we fail.

Even then, my extra sense, the one that's only for Giulio, is on high alert and trained on the door, waiting and hoping for him to show up. But he hasn't. Not yet.

'I barely made it on to the last Metro,' Ma wheezes as she dumps four bulging IKEA bags on to the counter. 'It was packed – everyone rushing to get on before the strike started.'

Towers of stackable paper cups spill over the edges, and Ma slumps with them, red-faced from exertion.

'Hey!' I poke her arm. 'No time to rest. I've sent you a screenshot of Ren and Enrico's shopping lists. They're upstairs now. They even know where to find that special ingredient I asked for.'

Ma barely lifts her head. 'They're here already?'

I raise an eyebrow. 'Can't you smell?'

The aroma of Ren's fusion snacks and Enrico's Roman classics are already wafting down from Nina's kitchen. I swear it's drawing people into the bar – that, and the sense that something's happening here today.

It's barely midday, but we've been running around for hours already – since I bounced on to Ma's mattress at 5 a.m. to announce The Plan.

It's busier than usual for a Saturday, too – mostly because we've offered the neighbours free coffees for any folding tables, camping stoves and fairy lights they might have stashed in their basements.

I'm slicing a lemon, gasping as the juice stings the paper cuts I've collected from folding flyers all morning, when Signora Pedretti bustles in. 'Have you seen Giulio?' She leans over the counter, as if we're hiding him. 'I thought he'd be here by now.'

'There's a strike,' Ma reminds her, as if the echoing

chaos of car horns and angry shouts weren't enough. 'Nothing's moving. He's probably caught up in it.'

I shake my head. 'That's not it. He told me he had stuff to do today. And the strike wouldn't bother him. He's got his Vespa.' And he's probably on it with Flaminia now – the image of them together stings more than a thousand lemony paper cuts.

Signora Pedretti seems about to say something, then she folds in her lips as if she's thought better of it.

My love flu symptoms flare up with a vengeance, aching deep into my bones. She probably knows Giulio's with Flaminia, but my feelings must be so obvious, she can't bring herself to tell me.

39

'Left a bit... right a bit... higher... lower... there!'

Our bedsheet banner is perfectly centred above the bar door and I give Ren and Sofia a big thumbs up. This is it. It's official. Hours of frantic phone calls, speedy shopping trips, and begging at neighbouring doors and businesses, and our fundraiser – BREW COMMUNITY – is officially underway.

The banner, with its marker pen bubble writing, is as makeshift and scrappy as the rest of our efforts, but if I step back and scrunch my eyes a bit, the last-minute lively event that now stretches from the bar all the way to the fountain at the bottom of the street is not a million miles away from the Piazza Navona–Edinburgh Fringe Festival mash-up idea that kept me awake all night.

There are stalls and food and even a juggler in the shape of Kenzi's older brother, Mehdi – minus the fire, hula-hoop, unicycle and traffic cone. But still, he's good. The Swedish exchange students are handing out flyers, but instead of advertising comedy and theatre events like the Edinburgh festival, these ones show a simple line drawing of Pasquino surrounded by handwritten notes that read: *Save Nina's Bar*, *Support Your Community*, *Help the Little People* and, most importantly, *FREE COFFEE*, written in at least six different languages. We're trying to capture the essence of what Pasquino stands for, giving a voice to this tiny corner of the city.

We even have a giant cardboard cut-out of the talking statue surrounded by stacks of colourful Post-its for people to scribble down their ideas for the bar – what they want from their community, what they'd like to see. And Sofia is like a modern-day version of Pasquino, sharing our story on the crowdfunding page she's set up, amplifying our voices online, too.

'You're incredible, you know that?' I peer over her shoulder, earning myself a mouthful of yellow hair, and watch her fingers fly over the screen as she uploads photos from her phone.

She shrugs, bumping my chin. 'It's not so different from the retro flash mob I organized for my mum's birthday. And who doesn't love an underdog story?' Her hand glides through the air like she's showing me a news headline. 'Fragile old lady evicted by powerful banker while stuck in hospital bed.' She shoots me a grin. '*Clássico!*'

Ma catches the tail end of our conversation and we share a grimace. Nina would be absolutely furious to hear herself described as a 'fragile old lady'. And, to be fair, none of the elderly regulars who've shown up for us today fit that description either – this entire event, aside from Ma, has been pulled together by teenagers and pensioners.

But despite the joy and energy that fills the street, my mind keeps wandering back to one person. Giulio.

I can't stop thinking about him – where he is, what he's doing, why he's not here with us, and why-oh-why couldn't it have been a sturdy deckchair instead of a wobbly hammock?

Ma hands me an empty wine cooler and nudges me towards the stalls. 'Can you go and collect some of the donations?'

I weave through our pop-up market. Paper tablecloths cover stacked crates, turning them into impromptu stands. There's one selling the friendship bracelets we've been stringing together in every spare minute, and another featuring Pay-What-You-Can portraits run by an artsy neighbour – with a cheeky sample drawing of a bank manager extorting money from someone who looks remarkably like Nina in a hospital bed. The raffle table is overflowing with gifts from neighbouring businesses — fancy wines, chocolates and handmade goods all jammed together.

But it's the food that is the real attraction. Ren's fusion dishes are disappearing fast. Enrico's Roman classics — crunchy *bruschette* and plates of fresh pasta — are keeping a steady line. Kenzi's jad is here too, dishing out Moroccan specialities while he chats to Enrico's friend in Arabic as if they've known each other all their lives.

As I move between them — locals and tourists, old regulars and new faces — it hits me. We did this. My friends and me . . . in a few short weeks we created a sense of community and belonging where we had none ourselves.

And maybe, in a way, this is what I've been searching for all along.

I've spent so much time trying to fit into one thing or another — afraid of being too Italian, or not Italian enough. But maybe what I am is exactly what this place needs. A little bit of everything, a bridge between worlds. Just like the bar.

40

Signora Pedretti and her cronies flock to the bar at sunset for a free round of bittery-sweet Crodinos – the sparkling orange liquid is a perfect match for the tangerine glow low on the horizon. I'm exhausted. My feet are hot and sore from rushing around all day but, inside, I'm glowing like the fairy lights we hung around the stalls.

Everyone keeps asking about our target – how close or far we are from reaching it – so Kenzi and I make a giant poster and tape it to the wall outside the bar. We name it the Bar-O-Meter – a simple column with our bold goal of fifteen thousand euros at the top, and fourteen smaller notches leading up to it for every one thousand euros we raise.

We start spreading the word that there'll be a live count starting at 11 p.m. and people are actually hanging around, determined to see if we make it.

'Keep collecting,' Ma urges, sending me on another round with the wine cooler. 'We need every cent.' She turns to Sofia, pen poised over a notepad, ready to jot down the online donations. 'How's the crowd thingy? Any updates?'

I move from stall to stall, emptying notes and coins from improvised collection jars – coffee tins, old bottles of passata, anything we could find. My stomach growls as I catch sight of the empty trays and platters. I haven't had a proper bite to eat all day, and now there's barely anything left – just a few slices of *bruschette* grilling on a camping stove, and the last few skewers of *arrosticini* roasting over the disposable charcoal grill at the next stall. The sizzling lamb is so perfectly seasoned and charred, just the thought of it is making my mouth water.

I circle back to where Ma and Signora Pedretti are busy sorting donations. 'Feels like the peak's already passed. The strike's over, buses and trams are back on, and the food is running out too.' I set the half-empty cooler next to the piles of cash already on the table, trying to gauge how much we've raised. It's hard to tell, but it doesn't look like enough.

Ma reaches out to cup my cheek and I pull away because – *ew* – her palm is dirty from handling all the notes and coins. 'The ideas you've had, the way you've brought people together.' Her voice is a little thick with emotion. 'I want you to know that whatever happens tonight, I'm so proud of you.'

Heat gathers behind my eyes and I might actually cry. 'I'm not doing this alone.' I gesture at my new friends, to the stalls around us and the small crowd that's gathered to see if we make our target. 'The fountain musicians are taking requests in exchange for donations, and we never even asked them to get involved.' I swallow the lump in my throat. 'But . . . despite all the help and free stuff, this whole thing's probably cost us a week's earnings.'

'You're not alone,' Ma agrees. 'But that's because you've brought these people together, and you've led the way. I see so much of Nina in you, you know?'

I want to laugh but I'm still choking up. 'Err, coming from you, I'm not sure that's a compliment.'

Ma straightens a teetering tower of coins. 'We might not get on, but I still admire her spirit and drive. She never gave up on this place, and neither have you. And if it fails . . . we'll make decisions about the next steps together, like we should've been doing all along.'

Together.

I want to be happy. But the word feels wrong when Giulio isn't here to be a part of it. My hands curl at my sides. He knows we're on the brink of losing the bar, his home, and even if he doesn't know what's happening here tonight, how can he just disappear?

Has he already given up – on the bar, on us – and I'm the only one left holding on?

And then, as if the universe has decided I don't have enough to worry about, Bertolli arrives.

He steps out of a sleek black car at the end of the street and strides towards us with a smug, entitled grin that tells me he thinks he's already won.

'*Bene, bene!*' Bertolli rubs his hands together as he reaches us. 'Quite the little event you've put together. Very charming.'

Signora Pedretti mutters something unrepeatable under her breath.

Ma bristles. 'What are you doing here?'

'You know exactly why I'm here, Caterina.' He sneers at the Bar-O-Meter. 'Bit optimistic, no?'

Ma folds her arms. 'This bar isn't yours yet, Bertolli.'

He makes a show of looking at his watch. 'I've waited ten years . . . I can wait another hour or so. In fact, I'll help.' He tosses a fifty euro note into the wine cooler like he's throwing away spare change, and my fingers itch to empty the whole thing over his arrogant head, even if I'd then have to pick every precious coin back up again.

But before I can make that dream a reality, someone calls my name.

I swivel round, and there's Giulio, hurrying towards us, his hair sticking up, his clothes crumpled, looking seriously un-Giulio-like. My heart does this strange, conflicting little squeeze – relief that he's finally here, tangled with a thread of anger that he wasn't here sooner.

And jealousy, Inner Isla reminds me. *Mostly jealousy, in fact*.

'*Grazie a Dio!*' Signora Pedretti clasps her hands as if a prayer's been answered.

But something niggles at the back of my mind, not letting me relax. Why is Giulio coming from the direction of the Metro station? He should be . . .

My double-take is cartoonish. The space in front of his building, those narrow white stripes where his Vespa's always parked, is empty.

My stomach drops like a boulder. 'Oh no, Giulio. What have you done?'

41

The church bells chime 11 p.m., marking the start of the live count, and Giulio pulls a fat envelope from his pocket and hands it to Ma. 'I'd like to donate seven and a half thousand euros.' He smirks at the bank manager. 'I sold the Vespa, to someone who knows its true worth.'

That smirk used to drive me up the wall, but with Bertolli on the receiving end, I love it – the smirk, and maybe the boy too. He sold his nonna's legacy – something Nina had forbidden – just to help us save the bar. To help my family hold on to its own legacy.

Bertolli's own perma-smirk fades. 'You sold it?' His eyes bulge in his red face. 'Well, don't expect any leeway now. The deadline stands – midnight, full amount, or the bar is mine.'

Signora Pedretti snorts. 'Leeway? From you? As if you were ever going to offer that.'

Bertolli's jaw tightens, but he doesn't respond. Instead, he scowls as she steps up to the Bar-O-Meter like she's one of the showgirls on the Italian game show Ma and Pa watch in the evenings.

'*Forza!* Gather round.' She gives her calf-length skirt a flirty shake then draws a thick black line marking Giulio's contribution. Sofia's camera clicks away, capturing the moment. Ren lifts Kenzi off her feet, both of them whooping and cheering while the crowd claps and whistles — I don't know if it's for the show Signora Pedretti's putting on, or because, in one fell swoop, we're already at the halfway mark.

I want to grab Giulio's hand and squeeze it.

Yeah, right. And the rest . . .

OK, Inner Isla, this time you might be right, I admit, a stupid grin plastered to my face. But then it hits me — I'm standing exactly where Flaminia stood yesterday and he's smiling at me now, just like he smiled at her.

Ugh. I have to know. I need to Be More Isla . . . in a roundabout kind of way.

I lean into him, my voice quiet amongst the crowd. '*Allora* . . . how come you've been gone all day?' The question comes out sharper than I meant.

'It's taken me for ever to get back from the suburbs.' He holds his arms out as if to say *look at the state of me*. 'The Metro only started up again when I was already two stops away. I saw Sofia's posts and left a comment, but there were so many, I don't even know if she saw it.'

Another loud cheer erupts as Signora Pedretti draws a line at the ten thousand euros mark and does a celebratory shimmy – Sofia's crowdfund has pulled in a whopping two and a half thousand euros. I notice Bertolli out of the corner of my eye, and the tiny twitch pulling at the corner of his mouth.

We might actually do this.

It's the cash donations next and Ma shouts out every time she counts up another five hundred euros. But the line on the Bar-O-Meter is inching up slowly now, and the cash is disappearing fast.

Worry threads through me and I edge closer to Giulio. Somehow, the fate of the bar and whatever's happening between me and him are tangled together – both uncertain, both on the edge of something.

'So . . . you weren't with . . . anyone?' I aim for casual, but I probably sound as desperate as I feel.

Giulio's brows knit together, then his face relaxes and a slow smile spreads across his lips. 'Is that what you thought, Scotland? That I was with someone . . . a girl, maybe?'

Heat rushes to my cheeks and my toes curl inside my shoes.

He pauses just long enough to make my heart stutter, then says, 'I was.'

My eyes snap to his.

'I went to meet Flaminia. She's—'

'I know who she is,' I interrupt, looking away. How could I not, when she's all I've been thinking about? Her instant likeability. Her teeny, tiny little nose. The two of them together.

His fingers capture my chin, lifting it so that I'm looking straight at him.

'But only to sell her the Vespa.'

He cups my face, showing me there's more to his words — that subtext he's oh-so-skilled at. It was maddening in the beginning. But now . . .

'Oh . . .' I mumble, feeling a bit foolish. 'It's just . . . you were with her the other day . . . laughing . . . and she had my . . . I mean, your spare helmet.'

Giulio smirks. 'It's actually Nina's helmet. But tell me . . . Were you spying on me, Livia Nardelli?'

My heart skips a beat. The way he says my full name — low, teasing — hooks into something deep inside me. His tone is playful, but there's something else too, something that makes the buzzing street around us blur. After all the wondering, all the tension, the relief of seeing him here, knowing he wasn't with someone else — it's almost too much.

'Flaminia came to see the bike the other day, but she lives out in the suburbs. With the strike, she couldn't make it back to pick it up. And we needed the money today. She would have given me a lift, but she was already late for her summer job.'

A collective groan goes up around us, pulling us back to reality.

Harsh reality.

Ma and Signora Pedretti have finished the count.

'We're still fifteen hundred euros short,' Signora Pedretti announces, her voice cracking with disappointment.

A wave of crushing defeat rolls over me. It's not enough. Giulio's tan pales to ash. He sold his Vespa — his most prized possession — and it still wasn't enough.

Bertolli runs a finger along the crisp fold of a thick brown envelope before handing it to Ma. It's real. This is it. The repossession order. 'What a shame. This place has such . . . history. Now, as per the agreement, the bank will be taking possession of the bar. You can stay tonight and clear your things out tomorrow.'

Ren is standing in the doorway, his hands clenched into fists, and I see Kenzi and Sofia on the edge of the crowd, their faces taut with the same frustration and helplessness I'm feeling. It's like we're stuck in slow motion, watching everything slip away.

And then, just as Bertolli turns to leave, there's yet another commotion at the end of the street. It's almost absurd how people keep showing up tonight – first Bertolli, then Giulio.

But it's only a taxi, the driver complaining that our fundraiser has blocked the road ... only, a wheelchair is being lowered from the back of the vehicle.

42

'Nina!'

'Mamma!'

Ma and I rush down to the fountain, where Nina is sitting ramrod-straight in her wheelchair. Her leg cast is mostly hidden by a long, pleated skirt, and she's wearing a silky red blouse with a single wedge heel on her good foot.

'What are you doing here?' Ma looks at Nina as if she's lost her mind. 'You should—'

'*Tsss!*' Nina hisses through her teeth. 'I knew something was going on when no one brought me lunch today.'

I sense Giulio at my shoulder before I see him, and we share a silent message. Nina hasn't discharged herself from hospital . . . for food, has she?

'I got one of the nurses to do a little digging,' Nina continues, swivelling her chair towards the near-empty stalls and overflowing bins. 'I know what you've been doing, Livia.'

I gulp as she beckons me closer.

And closer.

Then, when I'm right in front of her, she reaches for my hand and pulls me down until we are Roman nose to Roman nose – her intense espresso eyes look straight into mine as she clasps my face ... and kisses me.

She. Kisses. Me.

My chest heaves and I swallow a sob as the kiss becomes a tight embrace and she whispers, 'I'm so proud of you.'

I taste a salty tear at the corner of my mouth. 'Don't ... I messed up. We didn't make it and I spent the takings and we promised to give the donations to charity if we failed and Giulio sold—'

'*Tsss!*' Nina hisses again, pulling back to wipe my tears with the pads of her thumbs. 'I'm here now. And we're not done yet.'

Chin held high, she wheels herself right up to Bertolli. 'You think you can take my bar?'

Bertolli scoffs. 'Unless you have fifteen hundred euros stashed in that wheelchair, I'm afraid there's not a thing you can do.'

'We'll see about that.' Nina spins herself around and joins the musicians who are watching the drama unfold with everyone else. A moment later, she has the singer's microphone in her hand.

'I never thought I'd have to ask strangers for help,'

she says, over a screech of feedback. 'But my bar is my heart. It's been my life's work – a place where I've met friends, shared stories and kept my family's legacy alive. It's where I raised my daughter ...'

She searches the crowd for Ma, who's smearing her eye make-up with a soggy tissue.

'But this bar isn't just about me. It's about something bigger. It's about the people who believe in it – people like my granddaughter, Livia.' Her eyes are on me now, bright and suspiciously watery. 'We haven't had the chance to grow close, and that's something I've regretted for a long time. But since she's been here, Livia's shown me just how much we have in common – how much I've missed. Her ideas, her determination, her heart – they've brought all of you here tonight.'

Giulio leans in, breath warm against my ear. 'I've known Nina all my life, and I had no idea she even had tear ducts.'

I poke his side. 'Shhh! I've been waiting years for this!'

'And Giulio ...' Nina continues, her gaze shifting to him.

I cross my arms and mutter just loud enough for him to hear. 'See? There you go again, stealing the limelight.'

His lips curve into a knowing smile, and for a moment, we're back on the rooftop – Giulio worried I'd replace him and me anxious he already had. It feels like ages ago.

'Today, he sold his nonna's Vespa – the one thing he loved almost as much as this bar – to help us stay afloat.'

There's a murmur in the crowd.

Giulio shakes his head. 'How does she know all this . . . she just got here.'

'For anyone who can give just a little more tonight,' Nina continues, 'I promise you, it won't be for nothing. For every contribution, we'll have something waiting for you at the counter – a coffee, a croissant, a token of our gratitude. You're not just saving a bar tonight, you're saving a family's history and future, and the heart of this growing, changing community.'

I brush the back of my hand against Giulio's, the way he brushed mine at the hospital. 'Nina's right, you know . . . you made a huge sacrifice today.'

Giulio grasps my hand fully and laces his fingers through mine. 'I had to make sure you had somewhere to keep coming back to.'

A mini fireworks display erupts in my chest and, for a second, I forget about the bar, the fundraiser, even Bertolli. All I can focus on is him; the way he's looking at me like I'm the only person here. And all I want is to close the gap between us, to forget everything else and—

Ma hands us each an empty wine cooler. 'Quick ... pass these around.'

The moment shatters, but the energy around us doesn't. People reach into their pockets, offering whatever they can. Others grab their phones to donate through Sofia's crowdfunding link, which she's just announced is still open into the microphone.

And right before the clock strikes midnight, it's Ma who takes centre stage, her voice shaking as she cries, 'We've done it! We've hit the goal!' She leans down to hug Nina and my heart soars as they cling to each other. Then Nina reaches out to pull me and Giulio into the embrace, and we wrap around the wheelchair in an awkward group hug.

Over the top of Nina's head, I spot Bertolli sneering at the celebrations before he slithers off, swallowed by the celebrating crowd.

I look for Signora Pedretti, expecting to find her, microphone in hand, milking her moment in the spotlight. She's been so involved all day. But now ... she's vanished. Does she even know we've hit our goal?

I'm about to ask Ma, when the musicians strike up a tune – a lively, joyous rhythm that sends a ripple of excitement through the crowd.

Someone calls out, '*Saltarello!*' and I realize it's one of those traditional Italian folk dances – fast-paced and full of spins, with everyone joining in whether they know the moves or not.

Giulio holds out his hand and I half-heartedly resist as he pulls me into the fray . . . because I don't know the steps, but I want to be close to him. 'What's this?' I mutter, stumbling over my own feet as he whirls me around. 'The Italian teaching the foreign girl some moves?'

He laughs, his grin wide. 'No! I don't know them either!'

We barely keep our balance as the dance spins us in circles. It's messy and clumsy but, for the first time in days, I feel light, free – like I'm exactly where I'm supposed to be, right here with him.

43

'Giulio! Livia! *Venite!*'

Nina's bossy command to join her carries over the bouncy rhythm of the *saltarello* and Giulio and I exchange brow messages before jogging over to where she's holding court with Ma, Kenzi and my other friends.

Giulio and I are both a little breathless when we collapse on to the ledge of the fountain, squeezing in between Ren and Sofia.

'This language swap of yours ...' Nina begins, and I think she's frowning, though it's always really hard to tell. 'I've had a complaint from one of my regulars ... and a demand for compensation.'

My face falls. Compensation? The bar *has* been busy ... but has it been *too* busy? Have we taken over ... pushed someone out?

'Enrico's insisting I buy him a new pair of trousers – your language swap has made him go up a waist size, apparently.'

Ren actually looks proud.

Then Nina's serious face melts into . . . well, a slightly less serious one . . . and she reaches over to pat my knee. 'I want to keep it going.'

'I promise it will run itself,' Sofia reassures her. 'I've set up a page and a chat and everything.'

'Your nonna has even offered Mehdi a job,' Kenzi adds. 'He needs one for his citizenship application, and she'll need help when Giulio goes back to school and you and your mum . . .' Her voice trails off, and there's a flicker of sadness in her eyes.

'Go back to Scotland,' I finish, looking at the faces of my friends and family. I linger on Giulio's last and longest. 'But I've got plans to come back.'

His lifts one eyebrow the tiniest fraction. *Go on.*

'I was thinking . . . when I finish my exams next summer, I might apply to university here, in Rome. And if you're OK with it . . .' I turn to Nina and take a deep breath. 'I'd like to stay with you. I feel like I've missed out on really getting to know you.'

Nina beams at me – actually lights up with one of the Botox-defying eye-crinklers she usually reserves for Giulio. 'I'd like that too, *cara*. Very much.'

'Great,' Ma interrupts. 'But can we discuss this tomorrow? We need to get you back to the hospital. What were you thinking, Mamma?'

Nina scowls. '*Nemmeno per sogno!* No way! Do you

know how hard it is to find a taxi during a strike, and a driver willing to pick me up from hospital? *Santo Cielo!* You'd think I was trying to break out of prison. *Comunque*, I can stay with Giulio – his parents are still away and the building has a lift.'

Nina doesn't even check if this is OK. But then, why would she? Hasn't Giulio been telling me all summer that the two flats are practically connected, and that he's drifted between them most of his life? But their closeness doesn't leave me feeling left out like it used to – if anything, it makes me feel I belong here too. With them.

Just as that thought crosses my mind, I hear a rumble that I initially mistake for my own stomach, seeing as I haven't eaten properly all day.

Then a blue Vespa comes tearing towards us, the rider's helmet plastered in anime stickers. For a second, I'm thrown. It's Flaminia. She's come back for Giulio.

But those wiry legs sticking out on either side of the bike can only belong to Signora Pedretti. She skids to a stop in front of us like a stunt rider.

'Couldn't resist making an entrance,' she announces, cutting the engine.

She takes off the helmet and hands it to Giulio. 'This is yours, I believe . . . and so are these.' She holds out the keys, but he's so limp with shock she has to press them into his hand and fold his fingers around them. 'Adelina called me when she found out Bertolli was pressuring you for it.'

Nina sniffs. 'That man had as much chance of getting your Vespa as he did of getting our bar.'

I decide not to point out what a close call that had been.

Giulio's eyes are on stalks. 'But I sold it . . . to Flaminia.'

Signora Pedretti dusts an imaginary speck off the shoulder of her blouse. 'Because that's what we wanted you to think. We knew you'd sell it to help out, so we made sure the Vespa stayed right where it belongs. Flaminia brought it back after her shift. She would have come, but she had to catch the last bus.'

'But the money—' Giulio begins.

'Oh, that's real enough,' Signora Pedretti interrupts. 'But it's a loan, nothing to do with the Vespa. Adelina and I have already come to an agreement. A fair one without any tricky fine print, I might add.'

Only then do I realize the music has stopped, and people are drifting away . . . leaving an uninterrupted view of the mess that's been left behind.

Nina starts bossing Ma around, giving her instructions for what she needs from her flat. When they leave, Kenzi leaps to her feet and squeezes me into a huge hug. 'I can't believe you'll be staying in Rome! That you'll actually live here. We'll keep in touch no matter what, OK?'

I laugh . . . and gasp for breath a little too. 'I still have a couple of weeks left, you know.'

'Doesn't matter,' she insists, straightening, but not letting go of me entirely. 'You can't escape us, even if you tried. Sofia's already created a group chat.'

'Prepare to be spammed.' Sofia grins.

But Ren is uncharacteristically solemn. He places a hand over his heart. 'I'll share pictures of every new dish. And send you care packages. Something that travels well . . .' He pauses, thinking. 'Miso-and-black-sesame biscotti and maybe some—'

'*Forza!*' Signora Pedretti appears in front of us with a collection of boxes and bin bags. 'I had to call in a favour to get a permit for tonight and I promised we'd clean up after.'

The others scramble. Then it's just Giulio and me sitting on the ledge of the fountain, still thigh to thigh even when there's now plenty of room.

'So . . .' he says, stretching his feet out then pulling them back again as if he's as jittery as I am.

'So . . .' I echo.

'We should probably . . .' He gestures vaguely to

where Ren is packing up the food stall.

'Help, right?' Sofia interrupts with a smirk, throwing a couple of black bags towards us.

Giulio laughs and catches them easily.

'At least it wasn't your mum,' he whispers into my hair as he pulls me to my feet, his hand holding mine way longer than necessary. 'Want to meet up on the roof terrace later?'

44

I reheat my special dish in Nina's oven – relieved I forgot to put it out with the rest of the food, since there wasn't a crumb left after tonight's event. Ma pads into the kitchen, freshly showered and wearing one of my oversized tees, the one I've been searching for since we got here. It's a bit unfair that she borrows Nina's and my clothes, when we wouldn't find anything of interest, or free of cat hair, in her wardrobe.

She eyes the foil-covered dish in my oven-gloved hands. 'What's that?'

'Just . . . a little experiment. I'm taking it up to the terrace. Giulio and I are going to hang out for a bit.'

There, I've said it. And, weirdly, I'm not worried about her teasing me, or about being the cliché foreign girl falling for an Italian boy. Tonight, I feel like I've proven I'm more than that – to Ma, and maybe even to myself.

She must see it too because, instead of her usual cringe-inducing, no-filter comments, she simply says, 'Don't stay up too long, OK? It's late already and it's back to business in the morning . . . thanks to you.'

Then, just when I think we've had a breakthrough, she grabs me for a hug, her damp hair dripping all over my shoulder as she plants a kiss on my cheek, then steps back to give it a good pinch.

As she heads off to dry her hair, I carry my offering up to the roof terrace, nudging the door open with my hip. It's late – or early, or whatever it is when you haven't slept for thirty-six hours – and the air is cool and refreshing for once. The city is eerily silent too – that pause between people staying out late and people getting up early, when no one is around.

Except Giulio. He's very much here, leaning against the balustrade, watching me with a smile that makes my knees wobble.

'*Ciao*, Scotland,' he says softly, and I have to steady myself against the table in a moment of giddiness that has nothing to do with how little I've eaten.

I set the dish down and try to play it cool. But inside, my thoughts are a jumble – every glance, every smile, feels like it's filled with more meaning than before. This meeting tonight . . . is intentional. There are no more games. No more secrets.

Giulio lifts a corner of the foil, releasing a bold, savoury aroma. He sniffs, unsure. 'Is that . . . lasagna?'

'Kind of . . . it's haggis lasagna,' I explain, feeling like

I've just peeled back a layer of my own skin. 'A Scottish Italian fusion. Kind of . . . like me.'

I carve out a couple of gloopy squares, the haggis – peppery dark and smelling of spice – crumbling on to the plate. We don't bother sitting.

Giulio hesitates, then takes a bite. He chews. Then splutters. Then takes a long deep glug of the water I brought up earlier along with the plates and cutlery.

He chokes out a small cough. 'Will you be offended if I say I don't like it?'

I burst out laughing. 'Of course not . . . Wait, no, hang on – let me try it.' I scoop up a forkful, determined to defend my creation – but then I grimace, and reach for the water too. 'OK, fair. That is . . . not right.'

He takes my plate and sets it down with his own, then gently loops his arms around me. 'I might not like haggis lasagna, but I do like you.'

His hands slide to my waist, pulling me closer.

Then he looks around the roof terrace with a quick, exaggerated scan.

'What are you doing?'

'Just making sure your mum isn't going to pop up out of nowhere,' he says with a grin.

'Why? What are you planning?' I ask . . . not quite pulling off the joking tone I was aiming for.

A shiver of anticipation ripples through me as his (yes, Isla, you are correct) melty, chocolate-button eyes meet mine. He leans in, and I meet him halfway. Our lips touch, and – *sigh* – my nose bumps against his. Of course it does. But as awkward as it is, it's warm and real, and exactly what I want.

Ma and Isla's bet flits through my mind, and it turns out they were right after all – my first French kiss is Italian. It's like the rest of me . . . a little bit of a mix. Then Giulio's lips meet mine again, and all bets are off.

ACKNOWLEDGEMENTS

Crafting a book is much like making a lasagna – layers of effort, carefully chosen ingredients and lots of love. But, coming from a long line of Italian women, to my eternal shame, I can't cook.

Luckily, I didn't have to whip up this book alone. The amazing team at Chicken House were in the kitchen with me, getting their hands dirty too. Master chef Barry Cunningham, along with Rachel Hickman, Elinor Bagenal, Rachel Leyshon, Laura Myers, Esther Waller, Ruth Hoey, Jazz Bartlett Love and Emily Groom-Collis, all brought something special to the table. Head chef (and editor) Shalu Vallepur ensured my plotlines weren't half-baked and helped me shape this story into something (hopefully) rich and satisfying.

My deepest thanks also to copy-editor Kathy Webb, who smoothed the filling and checked for consistency. And to illustrator extraordinaire Ali Al Amine for creating such a beautiful cover – one that could proudly grace any menu.

My agent, Lindsey Fraser, has been the perfect sous-chef, taking care of all the extra details so I could stay immersed in my fictional kitchen. I'm also grateful for the writing courses and workshops that ripened and seasoned my skills – especially the Golden Egg Academy, WriteMentor and SCBWI Scotland. If they ever offer cookery classes, I'll sign up in an instant!

Huge thanks to my early taste testers – Emily, Onie, Sarah and Yvonne, who gets an extra shout-out for haggis lasagna (though I have no doubt hers was delicious!). And to the fabulous Write Magic sprinters for keeping me chained to the hob.

Grazie di cuore to my husband, Giacomo – my own teenage love story and the only person in our household who truly knows his way around a kitchen. Thanks to him, our daughters, Gaia and Thea, get to enjoy the delicious home-made Italian food I grew up with, much of which features in this book. And to them, along with my niece, Emilia, for being the next generation of third-culture kids for whom this story was cooked up.

I will be forever grateful to my parents, Bruno and Concetta, for Italy – for the roots, the language, the culture and the stories that shaped me.

All of these wonderful people (and more) have added to the flavour of this book, and I can only hope readers enjoy it far more than any meal I've ever attempted to make!

TRY ANOTHER GREAT BOOK FROM CHICKEN HOUSE

THE OTHER ONES by FRAN HART

Sal hates standing out. But he lives in a haunted house – and everybody knows it.

His oldest friend, Dirk, tries to help ... but he wants to stay popular, and Sal isn't helping. Elsie was popular – until recently. Now she's on the outcast's table too ... and she doesn't want to talk about it.

Then there's the new boy, Pax, who won't leave Sal alone. His idea of a good time is hanging out in graveyards. And, for some reason, Sal just can't stay away.

Meet The Other Ones. Can they banish their ghosts together?

> [A] loveable novel ... Perfect for fans of the Heartstopper books and TV series.
> THE TIMES

TRY IT!
READ CHAPTER 1 HERE

Paperback, ISBN 978-1-913696-32-0, £8.99 • ebook, ISBN 978-1-915026-07-1, £8.99

TRY ANOTHER GREAT BOOK FROM CHICKEN HOUSE

SOULMATES AND OTHER WAYS TO DIE
by MELISSA WELLIVER

GOOD NEWS: We all have a soulmate. Thanks to a gene mutation, out there somewhere is our perfect match.

BAD NEWS: Your soul bond means you feel their pain before you've even met. And if your soulmate dies . . . you die too.

Control freak Zoe is determined to stay alive – and single. She carries a survival kit for every eventuality, but even she can't prepare for a match with Milo Spencer, a boy who lives for recreational danger. It's time to find a cure . . .

Wry, inventive, and heart-warming all at once . . .
NADIA MIKAIL

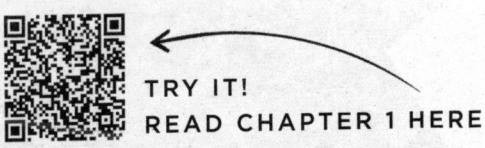

TRY IT!
READ CHAPTER 1 HERE

Paperback, ISBN 978-1-915947-13-0, £8.99 • ebook, ISBN 978-1-9159

TRY ANOTHER GREAT BOOK FROM CHICKEN HOUSE

ANNIE LEBLANC IS NOT DEAD YET
by MOLLY MORRIS

Every ten years in Wil's home town of Lennon, California, one person is chosen to return from the dead. When her ex-best friend Annie LeBlanc is brought back to life for thirty days, Wil's ecstatic – who cares that Annie stopped speaking to her before she died?

Discovering a loophole that means Annie can stay alive permanently, Wil has one summer to make things work. But first, Wil might have to face some difficult truths about their past friendship . . .

TRY IT!
READ CHAPTER 1 HERE

Paperback, ISBN 978-1-915026-77-4, £8.99 • ebook, ISBN 978-1-